NICO'S WARRIORS

VETERANS' REVENGE

Badger Wordsmith, LLC

Published in Wauwatosa, WI

MITCHELL NEVIN

NICO'S WARRIORS: VETERANS' REVENGE

Nico's Warriors: Veterans' Revenge is a work of fiction. Any resemblance to actual events, locales or persons, living or dead, is entirely coincidental, with the exception of crimes documented in the media. The incidents and dialogues contained in this book are not to be construed as real.

ISBN: 978-0-692-07862-4

Author: Mitchell Nevin

NICO'S WARRIORS: VETERANS' REVENGE

Author: Mitchell Nevin

Twitter: @NicosWarriors

Crimes and offenses—Untied States—fiction

"Men judge generally more by the eye than by the hand, for everyone can see and few can feel. Everyone sees what you appear to be, few really know what you are."

— *Niccolo Machiavelli*

CONTENTS

CHAPTER ONE

Zak Klatter sat hunched over, elbows on knees, on a tan metal chair inside the basement of Ascension Lutheran Church. His navy blue, short-sleeve Under Armour shirt gripped his farmer's-tanned biceps. In a matter of minutes the remaining thirteen seats in the circle around him gradually filled. A middle-age man with thinning gray hair, a spotty beard, and round glasses glanced around the room. "Luke," said the man, known to the attendees as Doc Moreau, "can you get the door?" A slightly overweight man in his early thirties stood up, went to the rear of the basement, and quietly shut a heavy wooden door.

"Looks like we have a few new faces here today, so let's get started. For the newcomers, I'm Dr. Moreau, the group's facilitator. My office number is on the blackboard. I'm here to listen and offer some suggestions, but it's really up to you to bring things to the floor. Most importantly, though, we start with an understanding that what is said in this room, stays in this room. If what is said here deserves additional attention, I will address those matters when they arise. We'll let those new to the group introduce themselves first. Who would like to start?" A well-built black man in his late twenties with a square jaw raised his hand. Moreau nodded. "Yes, please begin."

"I'm Xavier. I served with the Marines, Third Battalion, Fifth Regiment. Was supposed to do a seven month deployment in Sangin, Afghanistan in 2011, but only made it three months. My right leg was fractured by an IED, but I was lucky enough to keep all the moving parts. When I got back to Milwaukee, I had a tough time rehabbing and then finding work. For two years or so, I've had a lot of anxiety. I pace back and forth and can't relax. People I know say I'm just up tight. Hope being here and talkin' things through will keep me straight."

"Thank you, Xavier," said the doctor. "Glad to have you aboard. How about the gentlemen in the blue shirt. Could you please introduce yourself?"

"Sure, my name is Zak. I enlisted with the National Guard when I was eighteen. Hard to believe it was eight years ago. I was a member of a long range surveillance company. Got some great training, made some jumps, and saw some crazy shit. Nice thing about recon: our job is to see, but not been seen. The Guard phased out my unit in favor of UAVs last year. Can't really say I have PTSD. My problem is a love of adrenaline. For me, the rush was the most powerful thing I've ever experienced. Now, I'm having some problems falling asleep at night and, as my dad would say, 'transitioning to civilian life.' That's why I'm here."

"Thank you, Zak," said Moreau. "And you're right, adrenaline is like a drug. It has to do with the release of dopamine in the brain, which leads sensation seekers, like addicts, wanting more and more. So, in a sense, you're going through withdrawals. That's okay, and I'm sure some of the experiences others will share here will help. Who would like to start?" The only woman in the room raised her hand. "Okay, Mandy, go ahead."

"For the new people here, I'm Mandy, short for Amanda. I was assigned to Army Mortuary Affairs. Some of the things I saw, well, there's no way I could ever un-see them. The one that haunts me most, the burned remains of three men killed by an IED as they rode in a Humvee, I can't get rid of. Their faces were gone. Just some bone matter remained. I knew one of them, although I couldn't recognize him," she said pensively. "When I got home, my parents instantly noticed that I had changed. I was emotionally detached. It took just three weeks for my fiancée to walk away. It's been almost a year-and-a-half now. It does seem the longer I'm away from it all the better things get. The nightmares are beginning to subside. Still, I haven't been able to maintain a relationship. Seems no one I meet wants to hear about how I feel. The only people that do are in this room."

For the next hour-and-a-half members of the group listened to each other's problems. While in the confines of this room, the thirteen men and one woman felt comfortable in their own skin. Here, everyone could somehow relate.

Doc. Moreau glanced at the wall clock above the door. "It seems we're past time. I would say this was a very productive group tonight. If you would like, feel free to fall back on others in the group for support or, if things begin to go sideways, contact the VA or my office. The numbers are on the board. Hang in there and I'll see you in a couple of weeks."

When Zak and Xavier stood up from their chairs, a man in a

black Harley-Davidson t-shirt stepped in front of them. "In case you didn't catch my name, I'm Raul. After group, those of us without AODA issues walk down the street to Matty's for a couple of beers. If you'd like to tag along, you're welcome."

Zak and Xavier looked at each other. "Sure, why not," Zak replied.

———

Matty's was nothing to write home about. The small, brick bar on Vliet Street had ten bar stools, two tables, a pool table, a dart board, and cheap tap beer. When Zak and Xavier entered, Raul waved them over to a corner table. "Pull up a chair. I'm going to grab a couple of pitchers."

A half-minute later, the stocky, former sailor returned, began to fill the empty glasses, and offered some advice. "From going to group, you'll see why it's important to stick together. Employers will bullshit you, you know, veteran this and veteran that. In the back of their heads, though, a lot of people think vets have a screw loose. What are you two doing for work?"

Zak piped up first. "I had a job working at a sheet metal fabrication plant. It wasn't bad, but it was just too damn boring. Metal in, fabricated sheet metal out. I worked on the loading dock. I lasted four months. I just bought a property on North Avenue to renovate and rent."

"Did you get a loan from the VA?" Raul asked.

"No, my uncle loaned me most of the money. The rest I scratched together from my life savings."

"Cool." Raul turned to Xavier. "How about you? You workin'?"

"Yeah, I took what I could get. I'm a custodian at the university. I thinking about takin' some classes at night."

"So what you doing for work, Raul?" Zak asked.

"I'm a lead short order cook. I work a Maxine's on South 27th Street. Can't complain. After all, being Navy EOD (explosive ordnance disposal officer), my rate didn't exactly translate into much civilian-wise, unless I wanted to be a cop."

"When I got out," Zak added. "I took the Milwaukee police test. Made it most of the way through, too."

"What happened?" Xavier asked.

"When I got home from work one day, my mom told me there was a letter from the City of Milwaukee on the dining room table. She pretended to keep busy in the kitchen while I opened the envelope. After a minute or so, she poked her head around the corner and asked about the letter, which said I had failed the psychological exam."

"D-a-m-n," Xavier mumbled.

"When my dad got home, he said there had to be some way to appeal the findings. He kept going on and on about trying to pull some strings. Finally, I said, "It's over. Let it go." He looked surprised. Then I told him, "Dad, I worked for the government for eight years. These idiots can't get anything right. They got us involved in two wars, didn't have the political will to win, and yet, we're still there. The government fleeced $2 trillion from Social Security, and now they want to cut benefits. But failing me in the psychological exam, well, it's the first damn thing the government ever got right."

Raul had a confused look on his face. "So what you're sayin' is you really didn't want to become a cop."

"Yes and no," Zak explained. "I'm not saying I didn't want the job. I just don't think I would have had the patience for it. Right after New Year's, I was watching the news and some guy barricaded himself in a home on the south side. It was cold out, and the cops were all bundled up. They called out a county bus so the SWAT team could stay warm. Here you had a guy sitting inside his warm home, probably drinking beer, and watching the cops freeze their asses off. Me, I would have said 'screw this,' and went inside armed to the teeth to confront the guy."

Xavier chuckled. "Man, you're damn lucky you flunked that psychological test."

The three shared a collective laugh and a few more pitchers of beer. An hour-and-a-half later, the three men stepped from the tavern. "See you guys next week," said Raul, as he walked towards a battered, blue pick-up truck.

Zak extended his right hand. "Later, Xavier. Nice meetin' you, man."

Xavier looked down at Zak's hands, but didn't see a set of car keys. "You got a ride?"

"Not right now. My license got suspended for thirty days. My uncle asked me to check on his place on Pewaukee Lake while he was on vacation. I got bored and took his Porsche for a ride. Got clocked doing a hundred-and-ten in a seventy. The state trooper radioed ahead. They had a couple squads waiting for me."

Xavier laughed. "You're crazy, man. If you want, I can give you a lift. I live over at 59th and Chambers."

"Thanks, but the walk will do me good. It'll give me a chance to clear my head."

"Alright, man. See you next week. Keep it real."

As Xavier entered an older model red Dodge Durango, Zak walked a block west to Hawley Road and began the mile-long trek north. It was a warm, quiet night. A few window air conditioners from homes adjacent to the sidewalk collectively hummed in unison. Crossing West Washington Boulevard, Zak thought about his high school sweetheart heart, Katie, who had resided a few blocks to the east. The two had gradually drifted apart after Zak enlisted in the National Guard. Through a friend and social media, he learned Katie had graduated from St. Norbert's College, was engaged, and relocated to Appleton, a city in Wisconsin's Fox River Valley. Their first kiss took place on her front porch after their first date. *Things have changed so much since then*, Zak thought. *We didn't have a care in the world*.

Off in the distance, a whaling siren could be heard coming from the north. The siren quickly grew louder. As Zak approached West Garfield Avenue, he saw a dark-colored sedan being pursued by a black and white Milwaukee police cruiser. As the fleeing car approached, a duffel bag was flung from the rear passenger's side window. The cloth bag bounced off a postage stamp-sized lawn and came to a rest near the steps of a home's front porch. The sedan continued south on 55th Street with the police cruiser still in pursuit.

Zak crossed from the east to west side of the street, went directly to the duffel bag, and took a knee. He depressed a black clip, opened the bag, and, with the use of a light from his cell phone, examined the contents. Inside, he saw a pile of cash. He grabbed the bag and quickly ducked into a dark gangway. A few seconds later, he heard the door of a nearby home open. Peering around the corner, Zak saw a middle-aged, white man with shaggy, brown hair standing on a second story porch. The man put his hands on a thick, wooden railing, scanned the block, and listened. A minute later, the curious George reentered the flat and closed the door behind him.

Zak flung the duffel bag over his shoulder and quietly made his way to an alley behind the home. He followed the backstreet to a series of buildings behind those that fronted West North Avenue to the south, then followed another alley west to a series of homes that abutted North 58th Street. He cut through a yard and walked the sidewalk to the building he owned a half-block north.

Police Officer Denarius Blount chased a teenager through an opening into Calvary Cemetery. The slender, fleet-of-foot car thief had bailed out of a black Audi sedan a half block earlier. Blount scanned the dark graveyard with a 2,500 Lumen high-tech flashlight. Although the lamp could throw a beam a thousand feet, the low-lying ground fog limited the flashlight's effectiveness. To his left, Blount's eyes caught some movement. Crouched down behind a tombstone was a male clad in a black shirt. "Police, get on the ground!" When the car thief sprung up to his feet, Blount grabbed the teenager by the scruff of his neck and forced him to the ground. Seconds later, another officer arrived and held the suspect's left arm as Blount slapped on a set of handcuffs.

Blount reached for his handy-talkie. "Driver in custody in Calvary Cemetery. Two other black males fled on foot south on five-four."

The officers lifted the teenager from his feet and searched his person. "I saw one of your boys toss something from the car," Blount told the teenager. "There's a lot of little kids living in that neighborhood. If there's a gun layin' somewhere, I need to know before a little kid finds it."

"I don't know what you all talkin' about. I ain't answerin' shit.

Just take my ass to jail."

Blount walked the teenager to another officer's cruiser, placed him in the back seat, and closed the door. "Before I go downtown," Blount told his colleague, "I'm going to check the yards near five-five and Garfield. They tossed something from the car."

———

Khalil Jackson gasped for air. Having run a mile-and-a-half the one-time high school football player was winded. Ten minutes earlier, he had bailed out of a black Audi driven by fellow gang member Marcus "Mobie" Webster. After catching his breath, Jackson frantically searched a series of front lawns on the east side on North 55th Street. *Shit*, he thought, *it's gotta be here somewhere.* The "it" was a green duffel bag containing $100,000 and a kilo of cocaine that Jackson, Webster, and another co-conspirator had procured during a drug rip. Seeing nothing, Jackson caught a glimpse of an approaching police cruiser, ducked into a yard, and disappeared.

———

Inside his second story, two-bedroom apartment in an otherwise vacant building, Zak Klatter donned a pair of work gloves left behind by the building's previous owner. For about an hour, he carefully removed, counted, and stacked $20 bills, which totaled $100,000. At the bottom of the bag he saw two chunks of cocaine wrapped in clear plastic. *This is dope money*, he thought. *No one is going to report it missing*. Then, a thought raced through Zak's head. While the money was lawful to possess, the cocaine was problematic. Tired, he folded the green duffel bag, placed it under his bed, and decided to deal with the matter in the morning.

———

On the fifth floor of the Milwaukee Police Department's Police Administration Building, Denarius Blount spoke with fellow officer Ryan Klein. "I checked those yards and didn't find a thing. I reviewed the dash cam video and someone tossed a large bag out the passenger's side window. The video also caught a glimpse of a white guy walking on the east side of the street. It was dark so I couldn't get much of a description. Looked to be about five-ten and fit."

"Think he took the bag?" Klein asked.

"Depends what was inside. And Mobie's not talkin'. The guy was on foot, so he's gotta live somewhere in the area. I'm going to ask the day shift to check the video from the businesses on North Avenue."

———

At half-past nine, a black Hyundai Sonata came to a stop in front of a tri-level home on the far west side of Wauwatosa. Zak Klatter stepped from the car, thanked the Uber driver, and retrieved a black backpack. Stopping just outside the garage, he entered a four-digit code on a small pad, which caused the overhead door to open. He was pleased to see his parents' cars gone. On a shelf to his right, Zak reached for a clear plastic bin, removed a dozen pair of work gloves, took the cocaine from the backpack, and placed the drugs inside. After securing the cover of the bin, he grabbed a shovel from a wall mount and crawled under a wooden deck attached to the rear of the home. He dug a hole, placed the bin inside, and buried the cocaine.

Zak then removed a folded duffel bag from the backpack. He walked to a black metal fire pit, placed the duffel bag inside, sprayed lighter fluid on the green cloth, and tossed a lit match inside. It took fifteen minutes for the fire to totally engulf the duffel bag. He then entered the laundry room off the garage, placed his dirty jeans and shirt in the washer, and went upstairs to shower. An hour later, an Uber driver stopped in front of the home, and Zak entered the car.

———

Gavin Fitzgerald returned to his unmarked squad car. Fitzgerald, a north side detective with Milwaukee's High Intensity Drug Trafficking Area (HITDA), had been asked by a lieutenant to search the video surveillance systems of a stretch of North Avenue businesses. The target was a vaguely-described white male in his mid-to-late twenties with an athletic build, who was walking on foot around 10:30 p.m. the preceding evening. The tedious search turned up nothing.

Fitzgerald was disappointed. For the past year, the veteran detective had spent the majority of his working hours investigating the 4-5 Mob, an African-American street gang. Four days earlier, an informant explained the gang's enforcer, Marcus "Mobie" Webster, was planning a drug rip. The missing bag likely contained the proceeds from the robbery. The vague description of the white male gave the detective little to work with. He was, however, hopeful his informant could gather more details.

Had Fitzgerald driven away ten minutes later, he would have observed a five-foot-ten-inch white male, with an athletic build, step from an Uber. The man in a black t-shirt and blue jeans carefully scanned the area before entering a two-story brick building.

CHAPTER TWO

Inside the living room of his still-under-renovation apartment, Zak reached beneath the molding of a white bay window and depressed a small button on the right end. After hearing a click, he slid open a hidden drawer installed by his father — a master finish carpenter. The $100,000 was stacked neatly inside. A similar hidden compartment in a smaller bay window in a bedroom concealed a Glock .45 Gen 4 pistol and five hundred rounds of ammunition.

After hearing someone pounding on the front door, Zak went to the front window, glanced down through an open blind, and spotted a delivery truck from Brewer City Home Supply parked in front. The new toilet and bathroom sink had arrived. He exited the apartment, descended a flight of steps, and met two men outside.

"Where do you want them?" asked a man with a shaved head and two arms plastered with tattoos.

"Just leave them in the living room," Zak replied. "The door is open. I can take it from there."

Thirty minutes later, Zak followed the two men from the building. As the delivery truck pulled away, he saw steam rising from the hood of an older model Ford Focus just down the street. A young woman paced back and forth on the sidewalk and frantically spoke into a cell phone.

The neighborhood, as his father had explained, "wasn't the greatest," which is why Zak had obtained the pistol and a concealed carry permit. Surveying the area, he spotted a couple of characters eyeing the clearly unaware woman. After locking the building's front door, Zak approached the stranded motorist. "Hello, do you need some help?"

"I can't believe this is happening. It's the day before payday, my credit card is maxed out, and now I'm going to be late for work. Do you know anything about cars?"

"A little," Zak explained. "Can you open the hood?"

The shapely woman with chestnut-colored, shoulder-length hair entered the driver's door and popped the lock. Zak opened the hood and was greeted with steady flow of steam. "Looks like the hoses are okay. My best guess is the water pump or thermostat."

"Is it something you can fix?"

"Even if I could," Zak explained, "I don't have the tools or the replacement parts. The car is going to need a tow."

"Oh my God!" the woman shouted, as her eyes teared up. "Is there a place around here I can take it to?"

"There's a repair shop on Bluemound. My dad's been going there for years."

"But how am I going to pay for it?"

"I'll give the garage a call. The owner knows my dad. I'm sure they'll work something out."

A look of relief came over the woman's face. "You would do that for me?"

"Sure. This isn't exactly a great spot to be stranded. How far away are you from work?"

"Just six blocks up the street on 52nd. I work at a daycare center. I'm Hailey. I didn't catch your name."

"Zak. Nice to meet you."

"After they tow my car, could you give me a ride to work?"

"My car is at my parents' house in Tosa, but, if you would like, I'll walk you there."

———

Thirty minutes passed before the tow truck arrived. As the driver hooked up the car, Zak returned to his apartment, retrieved the pistol, and tucked the Glock in the waistband of his pants. After donning a thigh-level Chicago Blackhawks' jersey, he returned to the street.

"Here's the location and number of the shop," said the driver, as he handed Hailey a piece of yellow paper. "Give them a call in a couple of hours and they'll fill you in."

As the two walked east on the sidewalk, Hailey seemed at ease. "Thank you for helping me. I was in a bad spot. So what do you do for a living?"

"I was in the National Guard, active for most of eight years. When I got out, I didn't care for the job I had. I used my life's savings to buy the building I live in. Now, I'm in the process of renovating the upper apartment. Don't know what I'm going to do with the lower business level yet. What about you? Do you like working at the daycare?"

"I'm twenty-two now, and haven't done much to improve my skills after high school. I'm getting tired of working crummy jobs. I'm thinking about going to school for hospitality management."

A few minutes later, the couple reached the daycare center. "Well, Zak, time to get to work. Thank you for all you've done." Hailey flashed an attractive smile, turned, and walked for the door.

———

Lying on his left side, Zak used an aluminum drum wrench to tighten a water line to the bathroom sink. He slid out from under a basinet, stood upright, turned on the faucet, and was pleased to see water stream into the sink. A cell phone on a nearby dresser rang.

"Hello," Zak replied.

"Zak, it's Nick Singlaub."

"Hey, Nick. What's up?"

"Not too much. I ran into your dad today. He said that you're back from the military, so I asked for your number. Just wanted to see what you've been up to."

"Not much. I bought a building on North Avenue in Milwaukee. I'm rehabbing it now."

"Cool. How about we catch up over a few beers at Perry's tonight?"

"Sounds like a plan. What time?"

"How about 9:30? I'll buy the first couple of rounds."

———

Nick walked to the table with two tap beers and passed a glass to Zak. "So what made you decide to get out of the military?"

"I was in the National Guard and really liked working in a long range surveillance platoon. It was a tight-knit group of fifteen. Our job was to glean Intel on the enemy in their own backyard."

"Sounds pretty intense."

"The training had a Special Forces component. On a couple of occasions, the Habibs came so close, we could hear them talking. Last year, the Pentagon decided to phase out the three LRS companies, which meant it was back to reserve duty and drilling once a month. I decided to let my enlistment expire. What about you, Nick?"

"I broke with tradition. My grandfather was a cop. My dad just retired as a lieutenant with Milwaukee. My oldest brother is a Tosa cop, and my other brother is a detective with Milwaukee. Me, I'm a refrigeration technician. Best thing I ever did. I make more than my brothers and don't have to work nights, holidays, and weekends, unless, of course, it's at time-and-half or double time."

"Bet your dad and brothers have some good stories to tell, though," Zak replied.

"Oh, yeah, no doubt about that. Still, I'm glad to be doing what I'm doing. So what's up with the building you bought? Must have set you back a chunk of change."

"It sure did. My uncle is one of the better known cosmetic dentists in the country. He loaned me eighty percent of what I needed. I poured my life's savings into the rest."

"Is it an apartment building?"

"There is a two-bedroom apartment on the second level," Zak replied. "For now, I'm staying there. I'm not sure what I want to do with the lower level. It's zoned commercial."

"Hmm," Nick wondered aloud, "did you ever think of opening a pub?"

"The lower level was formerly a small restaurant, so, yeah, I've thought about it. The business could rent the space from my LLC."

"It's a sketchy area, though," Nick warned. "Before doing something, you should give my brother, Steve, a call. He's the

Milwaukee detective."

"If I go that route, Nick, I'll do that."

———

On a sunny Saturday morning, Hailey stood at the front counter of Thompkins' Auto Repair. An older man with grimy hands greeted her. "Good morning, young lady. What can I help you with?"

"I'm here to pick up a 2006 Ford Focus. Last name is Chevallier."

The man searched through a stack of repair orders. "Ah, here it is. We replaced the thermostat and checked the hoses. Looks like the damage is $423.53." The man removed a carbon copy of the repair order and handed it across the counter.

Hailey looked through the itemized list of repairs. "In all honesty, sir, the cost of the tow is missing."

"We contract with a service," the man explained. "The cost is paid up front with the tow company."

Hailey looked perplexed. "But I never gave them a card number."

"The tow was paid for by Jim Klatter's kid, Zak. He put it on a credit card."

"I need to reimburse him," Hailey demanded.

The man seemed confused. "Well, if you're so inclined, nothing's stopping you from doing so."

"What's stopping me is I barely know him. He saw my car was broke down and came over to help me. Do you happen to have his phone number?"

The mechanic looked over the customer and concluded the shapely, one hundred-and-thirty pound woman was an improbable security risk.

"Alright, I'll give you his number, but this better be on the up and up."

Hailey flashed a smile. "I promise you, my only intention is to reimburse him."

The garage attendant ran the woman's credit card through a magnetic reader, handed over a receipt, and retrieved the Ford Focus. Hailey drove off, but, a few blocks later, pulled into the parking lot of a grocery store to make a phone call.

"Hello," said a male voice.

"May I speak with Zak?"

"This is he."

"Zak, this is Hailey, the person whose car broke down the other day."

"Sure, I remember."

"I went to pick up my car today and the guy from the shop told me you paid for the tow. Please tell me the amount so I can reimburse you."

"It was on me, Hailey. Next time you see a person who needs something, you can reimburse me by helping them."

"Well, that is very nice of you, but…"

"Look, Hailey, I remember you saying your finances were tight. I'm fortunate to be doing a little bit better."

In all actuality, Zak had been living hand-to-mouth before coming upon the duffel bag of cash, subsisting on a food budget of $5 a day.

"If you really want to pay me back, Hailey, let me buy you dinner. It gets a little lonely working here by myself all day and I could use the company."

Hailey hesitated for a few seconds. "Um, alright, sure. I can do that. I'm in the area now and have some free time."

"Good deal," Zak replied, as he cracked a smile. "I need to clean up a little. I'll meet you outside in 15 minutes."

———

Dinner went well and, what had been "some free time" turned into a two-and-half-hour conversation. "So, Zak," Hailey asked on the trip back, "what's up with your car?"

"My car is at my parents' house in Tosa. The reason it is there, though, is I lost my license for thirty days for excessive spending – going one hundred-and-ten in a seventy. I'm eligible to get my license back Friday."

"Hmm, are there any other secrets I should know about you, Zak?"

"No, that's the only run-in I've ever had with the law. Not even parking tickets."

"Good. Glad to know I didn't spend the last three hours with some hoodlum."

"I really had a good time tonight," Zak added, as the car pulled to the curb. "Would you be interested in doing something Saturday night?"

"Like what?"

"The baseball game. I have a couple of tickets. I was going to ask someone from the vets' group, but I'd much rather go with you."

"Sure," Hailey replied, "I enjoy going to the games."

"Good deal. I can pick you up at 4:30."

"I guess it's one of the things we didn't discuss at dinner. I live with my parents in Menomonee Falls. It would be easier for me to stop over and pick you up. No offense, but I would rather have my car parked at the stadium than on the street."

"No offense taken. I'll see you Saturday around five."

—

The basement door to Ascension Lutheran Church's meeting room opened and, one by one, those who had attended the bi-weekly veterans' group filed through the door. A handful of the attendees congregated on the sidewalk. As usual, Raul extended an overture. "For anyone interested, we're heading over to Matty's."

"Are you steppin' out for a beer?" Xavier asked Zak.

"Nah, I'm heading home, but, if you're up to it, I'm renovating my building and could use a hand carrying a couple old cabinets outside. The beer's on me afterwards."

"Yeah, I can help."

Once at the building, the two men twice maneuvered cabinets down a flight of steps, through a rear door, and set them down adjacent to a dumpster near the alley. By the time they scaled the steps back to Zak's apartment, the humid air had caused them to break into a noticeable sweat.

"Have a seat," Zak told his guest. "I'll grab a couple of beers."

Xavier sat in a leather recliner and stared at the fifty-seven inch flat screen television mounted to the wall. "Nice crib, man. I'd have never thought so looking at the building from the outside."

Zak handed over a cold can of Miller Lite. "I put a lot of sweat equity into this place. Plus, my dad — he's a carpenter — did some nice work. Sometimes, though, I get a little worried about the area. There's a house a few doors north on fifty-seventh I think is a dope spot. Lots of people coming and going at all hours of the night."

"Man, I hate dope dealers," Xavier opined, after sipping from the aluminum can. "Makin' all that money sellin' their shit. That's why I joined the Marines — to get away from that bullshit. Dudes just swooped in and took over the block where I used to live. Bunch of assholes."

"You think these dealers make a lot of money?" Zak asked.

"Man, if you could shake the scratch from their pockets, in Milwaukee alone, you'd be a multi-millionaire."

Zak sat back in his chair. "Hmm, that'd be interesting."

"What you talkin' about?"

"Shaking the money out of their pockets."

Xavier looked surprised. "You mean gankin' their asses?"

Zak nodded affirmatively. "I just wonder how tough would it be."

"I'm tellin' you, Zak, drug dealers take their money seriously. To do something like that, you'd need big balls, bigger guns, and good 4-1-1."

"The Intel would be a problem. I've never messed with drugs

and don't hang with people who do. But what about the low-hanging fruit? Can't be that tough."

"To tell you the truth," Xavier added, "when those assholes began taking over my block, I thought about it. Not so much gankin' them, but acting out."

"Like vigilantism?" Zak asked.

"Yeah, like the movie *Death Wish* — getting back at them."

"When I was deployed," Zak recalled, "I read a story about Nico Walker, a former army medic with a ton of string ribbons and badges. He was involved in two hundred and fifty missions in Iraq. When Nico got out, he robbed ten banks, mostly on impulse from PTSD. Probably his way of thrill seeking."

"He got caught, right?" Xavier asked.

"Of course. Got eleven years in prison. Kind of stupid, though, robbing banks. Think about it: First, he stuck a gun in the faces of bank tellers just trying to earn some extra money to help their kids through college or pay some bills. What do bank tellers make, twelve bucks an hour? Second, the employees at the bank are going to report the robberies."

"True that," said Xavier. "Sad, man. Dude's suffering from PTSD so he sticks a gun at people for what? So they can have nightmares. Kind of crazy."

"That's the sweet thing about dope dealers. They're not going to call the police and report they've been robbed of their dope money. And the people involved, they're shit bags."

Xavier grinned. "Getting ganked would be karma comin' back at them."

"I'll tell you what, Xavier, think about it for a couple of weeks. We'll talk more after group."

———

In a basement of a dilapidated duplex near 35th and Center Streets, a group of nine men formed a circle around La'trell "Boo Boo" Triplett. "You fucked up!" Marcus "Mobie" Webster shouted. "Puttin' that bag out the window, dog. You need a beat down."

Khalil Jackson threw the first series of blows. "Ah, shit. Man, ah, ah, I was scared!" Triplett screamed. The other members of the 4-5 Mob started in. Within a minute, the discipline Triplett was dealt, left the gang member — bleeding from the nose and mouth — lying on the basement floor.

Jeremiah "J.B." Barnes stood next to Triplett, kicked the defenseless man in the side, and spit in the injured man's face. "You're a punk ass pussy. Next time, it'll be the last time."

J.B. and Mobie walked to the far end of the basement. "Nothin' on that duffel bag yet?" J.B. asked.

"Nothin', not a damn thing. Don't think the popo got it. They never said nothin' to me about it when I was locked up."

"A hundred large and two keys in that damn thing." J.B. thought for a moment. "Someone had to hear somethin' about the mac (robbery)."

CHAPTER THREE

With a plastic sub sandwich bag in his left hand, Zak approached the front door of London Bridges Day Care and pulled open the glass front door. Standing to his left, Hailey said something inaudible to a colleague, smiled, and walked towards her guest. "Follow me. We can sit at the picnic table in the back." After maneuvering through a room of small children, the two took seats on the opposite side of the white-washed table.

"You didn't have to bring lunch, Zak."

"I had a good time with you at the game Saturday. Bringing lunch gives me a good excuse to see you." By the look on her face, Zak could tell something wasn't right.

"There is something I need to tell you," Hailey explained. "The day you helped me with the car, do you recall me saying something about going to school for hospitality management?"

"I do."

"Well, I've thought it over for the last two weeks and finally made a decision. I've enrolled at UW-Stout for classes and I'll be leaving Friday."

"Okay…" Zak sighed.

"You're a really nice guy, Zak. I really mean that. You have a lot going for you, but I can't be dependent on anyone. I need my own skills. This is something I've thought about for almost two years. I'm making ten-fifty an hour here. I want a real career so I don't have to depend on strangers to pay for my towing service."

"I understand, Hailey, but I'd be lying if I said I wasn't disappointed."

"I get that, Zak, but I don't want to string you along. Stout is two hundred-and-eighty miles away. I don't plan on coming back until Thanksgiving."

After finishing lunch, Hailey escorted her disenchanted guest to the day care center's front door. "I wish you luck," she said, "but something tells me you won't need it. You have my number. Keep in touch."

Fifty-two-year-old Jim Klatter backed a Ford F-150 pickup truck to an open garage door. The well-built carpenter, with broad shoulders and thick hands, removed a stack of lumber from the truck's bed. "Are you sure you want to go in to the bar business, Zak?"

"It's not just a bar. It's a pub: lunch, dinner, and just pizza after nine."

The inquisition continued. "Don't you have to get a license to operate?"

"All that stuff is in the works, dad. I have an attorney taking care of it."

"An attorney? Must be setting you back a few bucks."

"It's just paperwork," Zak reasoned, "and it's not as much as you think. Besides, you know me, I'm cheap. I make every penny count. The only reason I've been able to swing it is because of your help."

"I don't know, Zak. The bar business is tough work, especially in this neighborhood. But, hell, the way I see it, if it doesn't work out, you'll still have a refurbished property to sell."

"I've already thought through the clientele part. I'm going to call the place *The Fallen*, in honor of those who've died for the country — military, cops, and firefighters. I'll have framed memorials on the walls. That ought to bring the good people in and keep the riffraff out."

Zak had a strong hunch his father suspected the money required for the project didn't add up. In fact, most of the materials for the pub had been purchased with $30,000, in various increments of cash, from twelve different suppliers.

"I hope it works out," his father cautioned. "I'll be here at eight on Saturday to get started. If things go well, it should take about a month. Do you have someone lined up for the electrical work? If not, I have a guy in mind and he can pull the permits."

"Thanks, dad. I'll take you up on that."

With the lumber resting on the garage floor, Zak pulled down and locked a metal overhead door.

"Jump in," Jim Klatter shouted. "Your mother has dinner waiting."

Fifteen minutes later, the two men pulled into the family's garage. Zak opened the entryway door and walked through the laundry room. At the top of a small flight of steps, he saw his mother slowly stirring a pot on the kitchen stove. "Smells good. What is it?"

Gayle Klatter turned and smiled. "It's a summer squash and corn chowder soup. Could you set the table?"

Zak opened a cupboard, removed three bowls, and retrieved three sets of silverware from a drawer.

"Did you hear about Lilian Gonzales' daughter, Angelica?"

"No, mom. What's going on?"

"So sad. She died from an overdose."

"You've gotta be kidding me! What'd she OD on?"

"She hurt her back playing volleyball in college and got hooked on OxyContin. Lilian told me Angelica bought a pill on the street, bit into it, but didn't realize the pill was a time release. She was found dead in the bedroom of her apartment."

Zak shook his head in disbelief. "Man, I can't believe it. Angelica was so smart. One of her friends said she was planned to go to graduate school and become a physicist."

"Her funeral is tomorrow morning at St. Kenan's. Her parents are absolutely devastated. I would appreciate it if you would come along with me."

"Sure thing, mom."

"Thank you, Zak. I'll swing by your place to pick you up at a quarter to ten."

———

Zak followed his mother through the interior threshold at St. Kenan's, dipped his right index finger in Holy water, and made the sign of the cross. Angelica Gonzales' open casket rested at the front of a long line. Zak thought it improbable that the slender, athletic, and nerdy student could end up dead and soon to be buried at age twenty-four. Lilian Gonzales stood adjacent to the casket. Her husband of thirty years clutched the grieving mother's left arm. Now at the front of the line, Zak extended his right hand, which was met with a firm grip. "Sorry for your loss, Mr. Gonzales."

The stoic auto mechanic offered some advice. "Love your family while you have the chance, Zak. You never know when they'll leave us."

When Gayle Klatter hugged her friend, the two women openly wept. "We'll keep you in our prayers, Lilian. Our door is always open."

As his mother stepped away, Lilian clasped Zak's right hand. "I can't believe my little girl is gone. I hope they catch the person who gave her that pill, but it won't bring Angelica back."

Zak felt the woman's trembling hands. "I'm sure there's a special place in Hell for that bastard."

After leaving the line, Zak stood in front of the casket. He looked down at Angelica's pale lifeless body, said a brief prayer, and made the sign of the cross.

Angelica Gonzales' wake reminded Zak of a military funeral. When a person dies before their time, there is a lot more grieving. Standing near the bar at Rita's Tuscan Restaurant was a familiar face from the vets' group. Zak made his way over, extended his right hand, and greeted the man.

"Raul, how are you?"

"Considering the circumstances, okay, is the best I can do."

"Are you related to Angelica?" Zak asked.

"She was my second cousin. Damn shame. If I find the asshole who sold her that shit before the cops do, I'll snap that prick's neck. Fuckin' dope dealers. I wanna kill every one of them."

"I've got no use for them, either," Zak affirmed. "Getting rich selling their poison."

"It's easy to talk," Raul added, "that's what the politicians do, but nothing ever changes. Same shit, different day. Tomorrow, another family will be burying their kid."

"But what if we could actually do something?" Zak asked.

"Like what?"

Zak put his right hand on Raul's shoulder. "Grieve a little, and spend some time with the family. Then, if you're still game, we can talk after group."

———

Zak handed a beer to his father. The two men took a seat on an old, wooden bench just outside the building. A sudden gust of wind blew saw dust from their perspiration-soaked shirts. "The bar looks great, dad."

"It should. It took me four days to make it. I gotta hand it to you, Zak. You've stuck a ton of dough into this place. I sure hope it works for you. Any idea what you're going to do with the kitchen?"

Zak threw back a gulp of beer. "I'm still workin' on it. I should know more this week."

Jim Klatter stood up, tossed the can to the ground, and crushed it with his right foot. "Once you've got it figured out, I'll schedule the electrician. For now, I'm calling it quits. I need to get home and clean up. Your mother and I are going out for dinner."

With his father gone, Zak placed a two-by-four in barricade brackets mounted along the front tavern door. He walked into a rear hall, scaled a flight of steps to his apartment, and took a seat on a sofa. After logging in to a social media service, he searched and found the account for Ethan Alperin, of Milwaukee.

The two Wisconsin men met at Army jump school. Ethan, who had dreams of becoming a Green Beret, was one of the few Jewish soldiers Zak had met. Ethan's father had owned a small junkyard on Milwaukee's northwest side. He died of a massive heart attack and left his wife and sixteen-year-old son behind. Mrs. Alperin sold the yard to a conglomerate, which meant Ethan had to find another career path. He contemplated joining the Israel Defense Forces. When his mother voiced her objections, Ethan enlisted in the US Army.

To the soldiers who knew him best, Ethan was known as "Scrap." Zak initially attributed the moniker to the junkyard, but soon learned the real reason for the nickname: the tenacious soldier wasn't afraid to mix it up. At six-foot-one and a lean 185 pounds, "Scrap," as one Special Forces solider explained, could "really bring it."

The young soldier's dream of becoming a Green Beret came to a screeching halt on a sunny morning at Ft. Benning, Georgia. During a static line jump, Ethan landed improperly and sustained a posterior malleolar compound ankle fracture. His military career ended six months later with a medical discharge.

Having located Ethan's account, Zak typed an instant message. "Scrap, it's Zak from the Guard. I just got out. Would you be interested in having a few beers?" After taking a shower, he glanced down at the computer screen and saw a reply. "I bartend at Lester's Steak House. I'll be off the clock at midnight. We can get a table there. Let me know if it works."

———

Zak entered the restaurant's front door. He glanced at the bar and saw a familiar face mixing a martini. Besides having longer hair, Ethan hadn't changed. "Do you have a reservation?" asked a middle-age woman in a red dress.

"I'm here to meet Ethan, the bartender."

"Oh," the receptionist recalled, "I almost forgot about that. I have something reserved. Follow me." The woman escorted Zak to a table tucked between the bar and the main dining area. "Ethan should be finished in a few minutes."

Attired in a white dress shirt and black slacks, Zak — with the exception of his age — blended in well with the upper-middle class crowd. At the bar, a television meteorologist socialized with an attractive, well-dressed brunette. Seated at a nearby table was pro-bowler Gary Grunewald and his wife, Jeanette.

"Ethan wants to know if you would like something to drink," asked a waitress.

"Do you have Blue Moon on tap?"

"Yes we do. Would you like a sixteen or twenty ounce?"

"I'll take the twenty, please."

A minute later, Ethan appeared with a beer in each hand, set the glasses on the table, and extended his right hand. "How the hell are you, Zak? I thought you'd be a lifer."

"The Pentagon decided to disband the long range recon units," Zak explained. "Rather than be a thirty-day warrior, I let my enlistment expire." The two men took seats on opposite sides of a small, circular table. "So, besides working out, what have you been up to?"

"Bartending, obviously. I went to school for accounting, but I'm not much of a book worm. After a few semesters, I gave up. I'm trying to cobble together enough money to get my own place. The tips here are great, but the only hours I get are on Thursdays and Saturdays."

Zak sensed an opening. "That's quite a coincidence. I'm putting the finishing touches on a pub of my own, and need a bartender. I bought a building on 58th and North. I rehabbed the upper level apartment for myself. The lower level pub should be done in a few weeks. I'm calling the place *The Fallen*, for all the first responders and military personnel killed in the line of duty."

"Sounds great," Ethan replied. "Kind of an iffy area, though."

"You sound like my dad. Anyway, I wanted to run a possible business venture by you."

"Sure thing," Ethan replied between sips of beer. "I'm all ears."

"A few weeks ago, I read an article about a guy who found $50,000 in cash stuffed in a backpack. He assumed it was lost and called the police. It was drug money. That got me thinking: drug dealers couldn't claim the money. In fact, they have so much money, they'd rather let the fifty grand walk than draw attention to themselves. So, if someone were get their hands on a dealer's stash, the missing cash wouldn't get reported to the police."

Ethan shook his head from side-to-side. "You want to rob drug dealers? Let me ask you something Zak. Don't you think these people have contingencies in place to make sure they don't get held up?"

"I have no doubt they do. We'd need good Intel and a solid

plan; however, we do have two big advantages — we're trained and disciplined."

"When you say 'we,' Zak, just who are you referring to?"

"You and I, and some other former military-types. What kind of equipment do you think we'd need?"

"Well, hypothetically, if this type of thing were to happen," Ethan explained, "probably a .223 rifle to cover long, a shotgun, and three pistols. Each person would need level III ballistic vests, and, if need be, night vision. Throw in a few canisters of pepper spray, too."

Zak made a mental note. "It would probably be tough to get these things without raising suspicions, right?"

"Actually, it wouldn't. When my dad died, his attorney gave me the combination for a safe he had at the yard. Inside, I found eight pistols and two shotguns. He apparently purchased them — no questions asked — from the characters bringing junk to the yard. I have them locked in the same safe at a building my uncle uses to store boats. I also have two vests. I bought them for shits-and-grins from a regular here who got divorced and needed some quick cash. Lower-level night vision stuff is available at most military surplus stores. Getting a rifle wouldn't be difficult, but it would have to be bought privately from someone who wouldn't ask a lot questions. Like any other business proposition, though, I would need to know, what's in it for me?"

"One fifth of all proceeds," Zak explained. "We could launder some of the money through the pub, where you would work as assistant manager. I plan on offering one of the others a job as head cook. Still, based on what you told me, I'm one man short."

"If we decide to do this, I have someone in mind," Ethan explained. "I know a former Navy Seabee. We've gone shooting together. The man is a deadeye marksman. Plus, he has a chip on his shoulder. His wife left him for a drug dealer. The dealer paid for her divorce attorney, and his wife took him to the cleaners. In the past, he hinted that he would be interested in earning some extra money, if you know what I mean."

"Sure, I get it. So, are you in?"

Ethan sat back in the chair. "Give me a couple days to think about it."

———

An older model Honda Civic pulled to the curb. Zak stepped from the car and slammed the driver's side door. He spotted Raul standing just outside the door of Ascension Lutheran Church. "Zak, I've been thinking about what you said at Angelica's funeral. So what's your plan?"

Zak chose his words carefully. "Robbing Peter to pay Paul."

Raul rubbed his right index finger and thumb on the bottom of his chin. "And what would Paul do with the proceeds?"

"Paul would divide it with the other disciples to spread the word anyway they saw fit," Zak replied, "but we're only interested in the contents of the collection plate."

Raul put his right hand on Zak's shoulder. "Okay, man, count me in."

"Good deal. We'll talk more after the meeting."

As the group filed in, one person was noticeably absent. Zak wondered if Xavier had second thoughts or, worse yet, went to the police. Though physically in the church basement, Zak's mind drifted. Halfway through the meeting, he glanced right and momentarily locked eyes with Mandy, who flashed a smile. The meeting seemingly dragged on until Doc Moreau adjourned the group.

Zak rose from a metal chair, stretched his arms, and felt a tap on his right shoulder. He turned and was surprised to see Mandy. "Zak, are you heading over to Matty's?"

"I am."

The slender woman smiled, then gently ran her index finger down Zak's left arm. "Okay, I'll see you there."

Standing a few feet away, Raul's jaw dropped. "What was that all about?"

"Mandy asked if I was stopping at Matty's."

"I guess you either have it or you don't. I've been at these meetings for three months. Never got more than a 'thank you' from her after buying numerous pitchers of beer. Let's get out of here. I'll meet you up the street."

When Zak left the church, he spotted a red Dodge Durango stopped in the street. The driver rolled down the passenger's side window and called Zak over. "Xavier, you're a little late."

"It got crazy at work. A pipe broke and flooded an office. It was all hands on deck."

Zak placed his head into the open window. "Well, you didn't miss much."

"Hey, the reason I stopped," Xavier explained, "is I don't have your cell. I wanted to let you know I'm still onboard."

"Cool. I was beginning to think you had second thoughts. We're stopping off at Matty's. Mandy suddenly became real friendly."

"I don't know, Zak. She's decent looking and seems smart, but can't seem to hang on to a dude. You know what that means?"

A puzzled look appeared on Zak's face. "No, what?"

"She's gotta be nuts."

The two men shared a simultaneous laugh.

"I'm just having a few beers, not proposing. Are you stopping?"

"Man, I'm going to pass. I had a long-ass day. Just want to get back to the crib and call it a night."

"Sure thing, get some rest. In regards to the other deal, I set up a meeting at my place a week from tonight at seven. The rest of the crew will be there. Just one rule: no cell phones or other electronics."

After waving goodbye, Zak walked two blocks to Matty's. Having entered the tavern's front door, he spotted Raul, Mandy, and two others from the group seated at a corner table. Raul passed a plastic cup of beer to the new arrival. Mandy pushed her chair closer. "So how have you been, Zak?"

"I've been busy getting my new pub ready."

"Wow, you're opening your own place?" Raul asked.

"Yes, and I need a full-time short-order chef."

"I dunno, Zak. I'm doing okay at Maxine's."

"I'm paying $17 an hour. It's ten hours a day, five days a week. That's $255 just in overtime. Mondays and Tuesday off. But I need an answer. The kitchen hardware is set to arrive next week."

"When would I start?"

"In two weeks. If you take the job, you can hire a couple of cooks to staff the kitchen. I'll even give you a title: culinary manager."

Raul's eyes looked upward. "Can I take a day or two to think it over?"

"Sure thing," Zak replied, confident his offer would suffice. "Why don't you stop on by tomorrow and I'll show you the place."

Mandy stared at Zak and winked. "Think I could get a look at the place tonight?"

"Ah…sure," Zak stammered. "The place could use a woman's touch."

As the morning sun seeped through cracks in the blinds, Zak's eyes gradually opened. The events from the previous night slowly registered. After gently lifting his right arm, Zak patted the other side of the bed, and felt a small body. *Hmm,* he thought, *Mandy's still here.* When Zak rolled over, Mandy lifted her head from the pillow. "Wow, Zak, you're a real tiger." She rolled out of bed in the buff and reached for a stack of clothes on the hardwood floor. "I need to get home and get ready for work."

"If you leave your number," Zak asked, "I'll call you later."

"How about if I see you at the next meeting," Mandy replied, as she slipped on her bra. "You're a good lover, Zak, but let's leave it at that for now. I need to run. I'll let myself out."

CHAPTER FOUR

Zak hung a framed photograph of Milwaukee Air Force Medal of Honor recipient Lance Sijan on the wall. He heard a knock on the front door, looked through a small window, and opened the door. "Come on in, Scrap."

"Wow, the pub is looking good."

"Now that Raul is onboard, the kitchen should be up and running soon," Zak explained, as the two men took a seat at a square table. "The place should be ready to roll in about a week."

"Is Raul on our team, too?"

Zak nodded affirmatively. "A Navy ordnance disposal guy. His second cousin just OD'd, so his heart is in the right place. What do you have on the agenda for the meeting tomorrow?"

Ethan opened a note book. "Did you buy the five throw away phones?"

"Yes, and I registered them at a coffee shop from an untraceable refurbished computer."

"The guy I'm bringing onboard, Dwyer Provost," Ethan explained, "is the former Seabee. He owns a closet full of digital photography equipment, which will come in handy for surveillance. He also located a party willing to part with their AR. We'll need to procure that as soon as possible. What about Intel? Do you have any prospects?"

"Xavier has a contact," Zak explained. "He wants to bounce it off of us at the meeting."

"Once we get a bead on a target and learn the landscape, we can train at a warehouse where my uncle stores boats," Ethan offered. "I'm in charge of the place, and have twenty-four seven access. The important thing is taking baby steps, not biting off more than we can chew, and making the risk worth the reward."

Zak leaned forward. "I agree. I've told all the others about the no-cell-phone rule, too. When I was home on leave last year, I ran into one of our guys from the Guard who worked inside the police department's fusion center downtown. Over a few beers, he explained some of the big brother stuff they can do. Most of it involves cell phones and social media."

Ethan laughed. "Gathering Intel on those who gather Intel. I like it. No doubt, that'll come in handy."

———

Inside of Zak's apartment, five men sat along the sides of a small kitchen table. The host placed a bottle of Blue Moon beer in front of each guest. "Look," Zak explained, "this is serious business and isn't for the faint of heart. If anyone wants out now, I'll understand." Xavier, Raul, Ethan, and Dwyer glanced at each other, but none so much as flinched. "Good, so we're all on the same page then." Zak handed name tags to each man. "Put these on your shirts and commit them to memory." Ethan became Jerry, Xavier's tag read Kramer, Zak transitioned to Elaine, Raul to George, and Dwyer to Newman. "Each of you will get a phone with numbers programmed to correspond with these characters."

"Why these characters," Dwyer asked, "and not those from *The Office*?"

"There's a method to the madness," Zak explained. "This is a show my parents identify with. If, God forbid, the police get their hands on one of these phones, they'll likely suspect someone in their fifties. It's just another way to throw them off our scent."

"Communication is key," Ethan told the group, "so listen up."

Zak handed each man a black cellular telephone. "None of us will ever call a member of the team on their personal cell phones. Do not bring cell phones to any meetings or take them along on any op. These are the only phones we will use to communicate. The text message feature has been disabled. Do not text from these phones. Do not leave voice mails. Use these phones to communicate with members of the team only. The location services feature has also been disabled. Turn these phones on each day at ten-hundred, fourteen-hundred and eighteen-hundred hours. Any communications between group members will occur within ten minutes after the hour. At ten minutes after the hour, turn the phone off. Cell phone companies store the tower locations for about nine months, so try not to call from home. If need be, the police will get a court order to triangulate certain calls. In an urban area, the cell phone company can trace the location to within about twenty-five feet. You'll notice these phones cannot send or receive data. Emails sent to cell phones geo-tag the receiver's location, even if the email is spam. Any questions about the phones?"

"Yeah," Xavier asked, "will we be using them on ops?"

"We will," Zak replied. "So use them sparingly. If one of the phones, for whatever reason, is lost or recovered by the police, we'll dump the throwaways and get new ones with different numbers. Any other questions?" Zak scanned the room. "Seeing none, Scrap has the floor."

"For those who don't know me, I'm Ethan, although my friends in the military, like Zak, call me Scrap. Before we can move on a target, we'll need the tools for the mission. Our first task is to procure an AR. Dwyer has a lead on one. He's going to meet with an individual he does not know at a tavern on the south side. These sales from classifieds like Gregslist sometimes go south, which means this is an all-hands operation scheduled to occur on Thursday night at 2200 hours. Dwyer will get dropped off by Xavier a block from the tavern and, at the seller's request, will enter the tavern alone. Raul, Zak, and I will arrive an hour early. We'll be in a black conversion van and take photos of all people entering and leaving the tavern. We'll also take photos of vehicles and their license plates. Once Dwyer procures the AR, Xavier will immediately pick him up as he leaves the bar."

"Who's paying for the AR and how much?" Raul asked.

"I'm fronting the money," Zak explained. "It's about five hundred more than the open market, but it's a no-questions-asked type thing."

Ethan handed several photographs to each team member. "The tavern is on East Stewart Street, just east of Kinnickinnic Avenue. The van will have a view of both the front and side door. The digital camera is equipped with a Tamron telephoto lens, so we will be able to capture a zit on someone's face if need be. Now, does anyone have anything regarding Intel?"

Xavier placed both elbows on the table. "I got a cousin who runs with some serious hoodlums. He'd have some serious 4-1-1. I gotta come up with a good cover, though. Anyone got ideas?"

Dwyer chimed in. "Tell him you caught a case and the feds are gonna give you a rocket ride unless you feed them information."

"Good idea," Ethan added. "Tell him the feds raided your place. Someone ratted you out and the feds found a grenade you brought back. You're looking at five years, but, if you give the feds info you could get paper."

"Yeah," Dwyer added, "use the feds. Getting any public information from them is like getting water from a rock. Come up with some kind of a code name. How about Operation Greenback? You know, a new federal effort to seize dope dealers' money."

Xavier smiled. "I like it. Alright, I'll kick it with him then."

"Make sure it's a one-on-one thing," Zak cautioned. "Don't ever bring him around. We don't want him to know who we are."

"Cool," Xavier nodded, "I got it."

"Speaking of information," Raul added, "One of the cooks that works with me has an uncle who's wired into a network at a south side food store. He stops by my place once a week for a beer. I'll prod him for information."

Ethan stood up from the table. "Good, so we're making some progress. Okay, I need to hit it. Let's plan on meeting here Thursday at 2000 hours. I'll swap out Xavier's license plates with a few I've hung onto from my dad's old scrap yard."

—·—

The boards of the dilapidated stairs creaked with each step Xavier took. Standing on the front porch of a 40th Street duplex — an older dwelling in need of paint and other obvious repairs — Xavier knocked on a battered storm door. A familiar face peered from a window. A few moments later, the interior door was opened by a slender man with dreadlocks. "Come on in, cuz!"

The wider and more muscular Xavier clasped the man's right hand and gave him a hug. "Been a while, Mookie. Hope everything's all good."

"It is, bro. Step in the crib. I'm going to get some beer."

Xavier took a seat on the couch. Mookie returned with two cans of Colt 45, and passed a can to his guest. "So what up, man?"

"A lot," Xavier replied. "A lot of serious, deep shit. Man, I caught a case. You know me, cuz. I ain't never been in the system.

I need some help, big time."

Mookie's BS detector kicked in to high hear. Although he never graduated high school, the heavily tattooed, twenty-six-year-old had a PhD in street smarts. For the past ten years, the former gang member had bought and sold modest amounts of cocaine and marijuana, but somehow managed to dodge a felony conviction. Mookie was keenly aware that a person under criminal investigation was a possible police informant. "What kind of case?"

"Man, when I left the Marines, I sent a grenade back as a souvenir."

"No way," Mookie asked. "A live grenade? Dude, how did you manage to bum that?"

Xavier put on his salesman's cap. "When we trained, we'd sometimes use live grenades. Another dude and I were in charge of countin' the ones we'd use. When I thought he wasn't lookin', I put one in my pocket and upped the used count by one. Dude signed off on it, and I was free and clear. The day before I got out, I wrapped the thing in paper, boxed it, and mailed it to my mama's house. Three days later, the package arrived. I put it up so no one could find it. When I got my own crib, I took it with me."

Mookie sat back on a sofa, took a sip of beer, and asked, "So how did popo find out?"

"Dude that counted the grenades with me ended up in the hot seat for somethin'. He told NCIS he saw me pocket the grenade, but didn't say nothin' at the time. Somehow, they found out I sent a UPS package to Milwaukee. After I left for work, I got stopped. The feds had a search warrant, took me back to the crib, and found the grenade."

"How much time you lookin' at?" Mookie asked.

"The US attorney said five years. I got a lawyer. We had a meeting with the feds. They said if I had some good 4-1-1 to offer, and it panned out, I could get paper."

Mookie laughed. "What you goin' to give them, cuz? You're a straight up Boy Scout. You won't even fire up a damn Phillie."

In an act worthy of an Academy Award, Xavier began to choke up. "Well, that's where I was hopin' you could help, man. The feds said they've got this program, Operation Greenback. They want to put a crimp in players' gigs by takin' their scratch. All I gotta do is tell them where the scratch is at."

"You want me to snitch for you?" Mookie skeptically asked. "Seriously, man, what's in it for me, besides a hospital bed or a funeral?"

"There's money," Xavier explained. "The feds said they'd cut me a percentage as an informant. You could keep the money, man. All I'm worried about is not going to prison." Xavier began to tear up. "You know me, cuz. I'm not hard from the streets like you is. I don't think I'd do good in prison."

Mookie took another sip of beer and thought for a few seconds. "What percentage the feds given you?"

"Ten percent," Xavier replied. "All cash money."

"Hmm," Mookie thought aloud, "that could be like twenty-five large for just one stash I know about. Got one question for you. Who's your lawyer?"

Xavier had done his research and came prepared. "A public defender. A dude named Gary Smith."

Mookie shook his head in disbelief. "Dog, a public defender for a federal case? Man, I gotta help or your ass is fucked. Let me kick it for a few days, and I'll get back to you, cuz."

Seated in the front seat of a black conversion van, Ethan observed a Harley-Davidson Roadster pulled to curb on East Stewart Street. A hulk of a white man with a bushy beard stepped from a motorcycle. Working the digital camera with the zoom lens, Raul snapped photographs of the motorcycle's license plate and the Nero's Ignitor's patch on the back of the man's black leather jacket. Raul turned towards the rear seat. "Black Harley," he told Zak, who dutifully jotted down the information. "License plate AB 1210." The motorcycle was the third vehicle to arrive at the bar since 9 p.m. Minutes earlier, a white Dodge Sprinter and a beat up Ford pickup had parked on Stewart Street. Raul had photographed the vehicles, their license plates, and the occupants.

Just five-foot-nine, Dwyer Provost was a stocky man with a shaved head, a light brown goatee, and a noticeable half-inch scar on the left side of his face. This biker-type look, and two arm-sleeve tattoos, made him look the part of someone in need of a 'no-questions-asked' rifle. Although skeptical of letting him enter the bar alone, Ethan and Zak believed Dwyer was savvy enough to smell a rat.

At one minute to ten, Xavier's red Dodge Durango stopped a half block south of the Rusty Socket Tavern. Dwyer quietly shut the front passenger's side door, briskly walked thirty paces, and entered the tavern's front door. Two large, burly men with scruffy beards sat at a table along the north wall. Dwyer approached a heavily-tattooed female bartender. "I'm looking for Musty." The bartender said nothing, but pointed to the table.

Dwyer then approached the table while carefully eying the two men. "I'm looking for Musty."

One of the men stood up, towered over Dwyer, and pronounced, "Yeah, I'm Musty. You got the money?"

"Yeah, I got it," Dwyer replied, as he removed a wad of cash from his jacket pocket. "Do you have the AR?"

Musty reached behind a jacket that covered an adjacent bar stool and placed a plastic replica of an AR-15 on the table. A look of frustration appeared on Dwyer's face. "You gotta be fuckin' kidding me. This is bullshit. That's not an AR!" Suddenly, two other brawny men in leather vests emerged from a nearby pool room. The four men then formed a circle around Dwyer.

"You know what I think," Musty said in a low, menacing voice. "I think you're trying to scam us. You said you'd pay two grand for an AR and here it is. A wise man might consider keeping his word, if you know what I mean."

Dwyer grudgingly handed the wad of cash over to Musty. Another man then handed the replica AR-15 to Dwyer. Musty smiled and then said, "Glad to see we came to an understanding. Now, get the fuck out of here."

Dwyer went for the door. Once outside, he raised his left hand, a sign that the deal had gone south. After he returned to the Durango, Xavier quickly pulled away from the curb, turned left on Stewart Street, and passed the black van. A few seconds later, a cell phone inside the van rang. "What the hell happened?" Zak asked.

"It was bullshit," Dwyer explained. "Four knuckle draggers surrounded me and demanded the money for a toy AR. You've got the guns in the van. We should bum rush their asses and demand a refund!"

"We need to think this through," Zak replied. "Have Xavier park a few blocks away. Walk back to the van, but stay out of sight of the tavern."

"Alright," Dwyer explained, "I'll be right over."

A short time later, Dwyer opened the rear door of the van and crawled inside. "Those assholes really set me up. There wasn't much I could do."

"Dwyer, man, look at these pictures," said Raul, as he reversed the photo frames on the digital camera. "Which one of these dick-heads is the guy who punked you?"

"Stop right there, Raul. That's him. That's Musty."

"Okay," Zak nodded. "We've got him. He's the guy who owns the Ford pickup. Look, we can't just go in there and bum rush them. First off, for all we know there could be five more guys in there. What we can do is find out more about this asshole, like where he lives, and take it from there."

"So you're going to let the money walk?" Dwyer asked.

"Look, what they did was kind of slick," Zak explained. "If you were stupid enough to call the police, Musty would tell the cops you agreed to meet at the tavern to purchase the replica, and, when you got there, you gave them the money. Worst case scenario for them is the police convince them to return the money. The mistake you made was calling them from your personal cell phone. For a few bucks. Those bikers could probably figure out who you are and where you live. Do you really believe they'd simply let it go?"

Dwyer pounded his fist on the front seat head rest. "I still say we fuckin' bum rush their asses."

"My dad always told me," Ethan chimed in, "never made a decision when you're angry. Nothing good will come of bum rushing them. Listen to Zak."

"Believe me, Dwyer," Zak reasoned, "there'll be payback, but there's a better way. We may not get the two large back, but we'll make them pay ten times over."

Zak reached for a silver .38 caliber revolver and tucked the gun in the waist band of his blue jeans. "Ethan, grab the forty-five and cover me." Zak reached into a black backpack, removed a magnetic GPS tracker, and placed the small object in his right coat pocket. The two men exited the van and slowly approached the beat up Ford pickup. Ethan peered around the Dodge Sprinter, and with his hand on a .45 caliber pistol, watched the tavern's front door. At the driver's side of the pickup truck, Zak took a knee, placed a hand under the rear wheel well, and attached the tracking device. "We're good," he whispered to Ethan.

After returning to the van, Ethan started the engine and pulled away from the curb. "So, what are we going to do now?" Dwyer asked.

"I'll find out where the asshole lives," Zak explained, "and we'll take it from there. Right now, I have a pub to open in a week."

CHAPTER FIVE

Finally, it was opening night at *The Fallen*. Zak had quietly advertised the event. Invites were sent to representatives from the American Legion, Veterans of Foreign Wars, Vietnam Veterans of America, and the Civil Air Patrol. He had touched base with Nick Singlaub, who promised to reach out to his relatives in law enforcement, and visited with the owners of area businesses.

Inside, the pub had taken shape. The brown, paneled walls displayed fifty-five photographs of those who had made the ultimate sacrifice. Six, square, wooden tables dotted the barroom. Designed and built by his father, the twenty-five foot bar was bound to get plenty of compliments. The shelves behind the bar displayed various bottles of high-end booze. A station in the center offered fifteen different tap beers. Inside the kitchen, Raul and two cooks, José and Alberto, readied the grill. Ethan manned the bar dressed in a white shirt and black tie. At 4:30 p.m., Zak opened the front and side doors for the first time.

Five minutes later, the first five customers, Zak's father, Jim, his mother, Gayle, his sister, Kayla, and two of her friends from the University of Wisconsin – Oshkosh, walked through the front door. His mother smiled. "Oh my God, Zak, the place looks great."

Zak gave his mother a hug. "You can thank dad for that. This place wouldn't have been possible if it weren't for him."

Jim Klatter took a certain pride in his work, but deflected. "That and my brother's money."

"Don't worry, dad. I'll be sure to thank Uncle Dave. He promised to stop in after six. And I can't believe Kayla came back from school for the opening."

Slender and a few inches shorter than her brother, Kayla flashed a white smile. "I wouldn't have missed it for the world. I brought some customers with me. This is Marcy. She's from Kewaunee, and Justine, on my right, is from Plover."

Zak politely nodded. "Nice to meet the both of you. Please, pick a table or feel free to sit at the bar. Menus are in holders at the table. I'll send someone over to take care of you." The group of five chose a table for six. Within seconds, Anne, the pub's sole waitress, approached the table. Zak stepped behind the bar. He prayed his family wouldn't be *The Fallen's* only opening night visitors.

Soon, other customers began trickling in. The owner of the plumbing supply store down the block visited with two employees in tow. Tipped off by Jim Klatter, two mechanics from Thompkins' Auto Repair brought their hearty appetites. Dwyer and Xavier walked in together, waved to Ethan and Zak, and took a seat at a corner table.

Some faces Zak didn't recognize. Looking at the array of framed photographs along the south wall, an older man put his arm around a similarly-aged woman. Zak approached the couple. "Hello, I'm the owner, Zak Klatter. Is there anything I can help you with?"

"This memorial is very impressive," said the man. "My wife and I were just looking at the picture of Officer Scott Robeson."

"I was a teller at the bank the day it was robbed," said the woman. "Officer Robeson was killed by one of the robbers. I'm surprised a young man your age would even remember the incident."

"I was a little kid when it happened," Zak replied, "but my dad told me about it."

"Well, God bless you for remembering," said the woman. "Look at these walls. They're covered with the faces of so many heroes."

The man extended his right hand. "I'm Walt Brennan, and this is my wife, Judy."

"Nice to meet you, sir."

"So, Zak," Judy asked, "what gave you this idea, you know, to memorialize the fallen?"

"I'm a veteran myself, ma'am. I served some time in theater. I hung these pictures hoping they'd attract the kind of clientele — the type of people who get up every morning and make this country tick. People like yourself, my mom and dad, and my uncle." Zak pointed to another picture on the wall. "People like U.S. Army Specialist Michael McCallum, just twenty-one when he lost his life to an IED in Iraq. He grew up in Wisconsin, not too far from here. Damn shame."

Walt Brennan frowned. "It sure is."

"If you two need anything," Zak added as he began to slip away, "please let me know. I'm new to the business."

Zak walked ten feet to the table occupied by Dwyer and Xavier. "So what do you guys think?"

"You did it right," Dwyer replied. "The place looks great."

"Good crowd, too," Xavier added. "I can tell, lots of people like the respect you've shown the vets and the cops."

"After you grab some grub," Zak explained, "I've got something for you. I've been tracking the GPS data for a week on our target. Four locations keep popping up." Zak handed a small piece of yellow paper to Xavier. "I've checked each of them with on-line street maps. The location on South Burrell is likely his house. Stewart Street is the bar. Bruce Street looks like the gang's clubhouse. The last address on North Commerce Street is the cable company, where he probably works. Swing by the Burrell address after ten tonight. Check to see where the Ford pickup is parked."

Xavier nodded. "Got it."

"And Dwyer," Zak advised, "I know you're pissed, but don't do anything stupid. If things go as planned, that asshole will soon be in a figurative world of hurt."

"You got my word, Zak. No funny stuff. What about the AR, though?"

"Scrap is going to a gun show Saturday morning. He thinks he can pick something up. Call me tomorrow at one of the designated times with that info on the pickup."

Zak walked behind the bar and slapped Ethan on the shoulder. "How's it going?"

"It's getting busy, and I could use a hand."

When Zak looked towards the front door, he saw Nick Singlaub and two other man walk in. The three took a seat at the bar. Zak retrieved three coasters, placed them in front of the would-be customers, and extended his right hand. "Nick, I'm glad you made it."

"Hey, I'm glad we could make it. Been looking forward to the opening. This is my brother Steve and, to my left, my younger brother Drew."

Zak exchanged handshakes with the men. "Which one of you works for Milwaukee?"

"I do," Steve replied. "I give you credit for opening up such a nice place at 58th and North. The area, to say the least, is teetering a little."

"That's why I hope you and your colleagues stop in as much as possible," Zak explained. "By the way, all active duty military and active law enforcement, get thirty percent off any of our tap beers. If you could pass that around, I would appreciate it. So what can I get you guys?"

Nick went first. "I'll have a Summer Shanti."

"Let's see, Steve mused, "I guess I'll take advantage of your special and take a Blue Moon on tap."

Drew piped in last. "Just a Diet Coke. I have to work at eleven."

Within the span of a minute, Zak had placed the drinks and menus in front of the men. "So, Steve, Nick said you're a detective."

"Yeah, I'm assigned to south side gangs for Milwaukee HIDTA."

"What's HIDTA?" Zak asked.

"A high intensity drug trafficking area," the detective replied. "Milwaukee is one of a dozen-and-half cities that have one."

"Let me ask you something," Zak asked, as he placed his elbows on the bar, "are you familiar with a group called Nero's Ignitors? Last Saturday, I was picking up some supplies on the south side. Three bikers were behind me, cut me off, and passed me in the bicycle lane on Kinnickinnic. I saw Nero's Ignitors patches on the backs of their jackets."

Steve laughed "Oh, yeah, we know about those assholes. They call themselves one-percent bikers – the one-percent of bikers that live outside the law."

"Well," Zak frowned, "I'm glad I didn't give them the finger then."

"Nero's Ignitors," Steve explained, "is the worst of the worst. An ATF agent and a detective in my unit keep tabs on them. A few years back, eight of their Milwaukee chapter members were convicted of racketeering in federal court. It crimped their gig for a while, but the N.I.s have gradually bounced back."

Out of the corner of his eye, Zak spotted his uncle, Dave Klatter, take a seat at the table with his family. "Excuse me, but I need to say hello to someone." Zak walked around the bar and approached the table. "Uncle Dave, glad you could make it!"

"You did good, Zak," the fit, tanned dentist explained. "Glad to see my investment at work. By the looks of it, you can really stretch a dollar."

Zak pointed towards his father. "You can thank your brother for that. He spent a few weeks here getting the place ready, even cherry picked the electrician and the plumber."

———

At midnight, Raul ordered the grill closed, instructed his assistants to clean the kitchen, and stood at the end of the bar. Zak placed a tap beer in front of his lead cook. "Nice work, Raul."

"It got busy, for sure," said Raul, after taking a sip of beer. Looking over Zak's right shoulder, Raul spotted Mandy enter the front door, place a light jacket over a stool, and take a seat at the bar. "She's b-a-a-a-a-c-k."

"Who?" Zak asked.

"Mandy just walked in."

Zak slowly turned around. "Mandy, I didn't see you come in. How are you?"

"Just fine, Zak," she replied, "and a little thirsty."

"Cool, what can I get you?"

"I'll have a sidecar. That ought to get me in the mood."

Zak retrieved a bottle of cognac, a bottle of Cointreau, added some lemon juice, and shook a stainless steel drink mixer. He poured the contents into a cocktail glass, and set the drink in front of Mandy. "Umm," she said after taking a sip. "So, besides being a good lover, you mix a good drink, too."

"Well," Zak grinned, "thank you, and thank you." Mandy's bell-sleeved top with a white and yellow floral print quickly captured his attention. "You've dressed the part for opening night."

Mandy ran her right index finger along the top of Zak's left hand. Ethan then approached. "A friend of yours, Zak?"

"Yeah, ah, Mandy, this is Ethan. He's the full-time bartender." Out of the corner of his eye, Zak saw Xavier and Dwyer enter through the side door and take a seat at a table. He tapped Ethan on the shoulder, stepped back from the bar, and whispered, "Keep her occupied for a few minutes." Zak walked from the bar to the kitchen, entered the barroom through a set of swinging doors, and approached the table. "What do you have?"

"Musty's truck is parked on the street in the 3400 block of Burrell," said Xavier. "Been there since 2200 hours."

"I carefully walked around the pickup and scoped it out," Dwyer remarked. "It's pretty beat up and isn't alarmed. We also checked the tavern on Stewart and the clubhouse. Both have surveillance cameras outside. My hunch is the cable company does too, but, even if it didn't, there are likely too many people coming and going."

Xavier sat back in the chair. "What you got up your sleeve, Zak?"

"Let me worry about that for now. Have you developed any Intel from your source yet?"

Xavier nodded affirmatively. "I'm meeting him tomorrow."

"Good deal. Once you get that info from your source, we'll plan and train for the first op. Now, go over and say hi to Mandy. I'll get you guys a couple of beers."

Inside Xavier's Dodge Durango, Mookie opened a boxed lunch from The Crazy Chicken. "This is what I got, cuz. It's a straight up money house up near 104th and Mill Road. The brothers ain't keepin' no dope up in there. There's no customers. Just a straight up stash house. This is some serious shit, now. These are Trey Downing's boys."

"How do you know these dudes?" Xavier asked, as he jotted down notes.

"Man, I kick it with them over there once in a while. Dudes are board as hell. All they gotta do is sit up in there, collect money, and guard the shit. My boy Fenny be sittin' up in there and we'll be playin' video games, smoking blunts, and kickin' it."

"So what's the layout like?" Xavier asked.

"They've got two Pits. They're nasty-ass dogs. When people are over or they order out food, they keep them locked in the basement. Money is stored in a wall cutout behind the kitchen stove, which, by the way, don't even work. First floor is the stash house. Second floor is vacant. There are two dudes there twenty-four, seven. Dude who answers the door got a pistol close by. There is a shotgun up against the wall near the kitchen."

"Hmm," Xavier thought, "how much scratch?"

"Like I told you before, cuz, about two-fifty."

"Two-fifty what?" Xavier asked.

"Man, two hundred-and-fifty large. Mostly twenties, some fifties, and stashed behind the stove in the wall."

Xavier looked skeptical. "How do you know that?"

"I was over there last week, man," Mookie explained, as he gestured with his greasy hands. "I fed the dude a couple of forties and he told me all about it. Man, check it out: I've been over there playin' video games when dudes came to drop off money. I could hear them moving the stove and stashin' the shit in the wall."

"Alright, Mookie, we're going for a ride so you can point it out. On our way there, sketch the inside of the crib on this pad of paper. And, man, make sure you get it right. The feds are for real about this."

Opened just less than a week, *The Fallen* already had some regulars. The thirty percent discount on tap beer lured two dozen off-duty police officers from Milwaukee, West Allis, Wauwatosa, and the Milwaukee County Sheriff's Department to the pub. Zak also asked firefighters and officers to bring photographs of their department's fallen members for display. Just after midnight on Wednesday, Steve Singlaub, along with two other men, took seats at the bar.

Ethan placed coasters in front of the customers. "Good evening, gentlemen. What can I get you?"

"How about three, sixteen-ounce taps of Antler Light," Singlaub replied. The bartender reached for the glasses. "Coming right up."

Zak emerged from the basement with a case of beer, set the box on a table, and approached the bar. "Steve, thanks for stopping in."

"No problem, kid. Hey, I want to introduce you to a couple of guys. Zak, this is Alex Reyes and Garrett Marks. They're fellow detectives from Milwaukee HIDTA."

The clean shaven Reyes looked the part. He sported a dark blue necktie, a pressed white dress shirt, and sky blue suit. On the other hand, Marks, a stocky, rugged man with bushy beard and plaid shirt, resembled a nineteenth century gold prospector. Zak shook hands with the two detectives. "Nice to meet the both of you. And this is my bartender, Ethan. We went to Army jump school together."

"Were you two Special Forces?" Reyes asked.

"I was a member of a long-range recon team," Zak replied.

"And I never made it through jump school," Ethan added. "My goal was the Green Berets, but I bungled a static line jump and shattered my ankle."

"I was just a rank-and-file zoomie," Reyes remarked, military jargon for service in the U.S. Air Force. "I have a lot of admiration for Special Forces' guys, getting paid pretty much the same for busting their asses."

"By the way," Singlaub explained, "Garrett keeps tabs on Nero's Ignitors."

Zak feigned outrage. "Yeah, those bastards cut me off on Kinnickinnic a couple weeks ago."

"They're some real sons of bitches," Marks elaborated. "They have chapters in twenty-three states. I have a photo book in my car. Just out of curiosity, I'd be interested to see if you could point out the N.I.s who cut you off."

"I don't want to make a big deal out of it," Zak replied.

"I get it," said Marks. "I won't put anything on paper, just make a mental note. When I run into these assholes, I enjoy seeing the looks on their faces when I tell them what information gets passed along to us anonymously. It gives them the impression a thousand eyes are watching."

"Okay, sure," Zak said, realizing he might glean new details about the group, "I'll take a look at what you've got."

Marks stood up, left the pub, and, retrieved the photo book from the trunk of his car. When the detective returned, he placed the three-inch high, three-ring binder on the bar. "If any of them look familiar, let me know."

On the third page, Zak spotted Musty. "I'm pretty sure this is one of them."

"Ah, Derrick Romansky," said Marks, "a.k.a. Musty 1%er. He's a real beauty. Beat the shit out of a striper about a year ago after she refused to give him a blow job gratis. Fearful of retaliation, she never filed a complaint. See anyone else you recognize?"

Zak slowly turned the pages. He carefully searched for faces Dwyer had identified from the surveillance photos taken during the botched gun buy on Stewart Street. On the next to last page, he pointed to another bearded man. "I'm almost positive this is the guy who cut me off."

"Interesting," said Marks. "That's Jimmy Delaforo, a.k.a. Piss Ant. The word is that he's the club's bomb maker."

"Bomb maker?" Ethan asked.

Marks nodded affirmatively. "These assholes take this biker shit seriously. They've mellowed a little since the passage of the *Patriot Act*, but, when the need arises, they'll do what they gotta do. With the prison sentences getting longer, fewer of these thugs are willing to take the risk, though."

"Funny thing," Zak added, "I've never heard of Nero's Ignitors before,"

"Probably because you're not a white trash hoodlum," said Marks. "They hang out at bars with the street-level criminal element."

Zak looked to Alex Reyes. "So what gang do you monitor?"

"I'm a financial crimes detective," Reyes explained. "I follow the money."

"You certainly dress the part," Ethan added. "Very professional."

"Well, thank you. I deal with a lot of financial institutions and accountants."

"No matter how much Alex tries to downplay his role at HIT-DA," said Singlaub, "he's one of the most important investigators. Some of the federal cases we put on these dope dealers involve money laundering and tax evasion. Alex, along with one of the IRS agents, nails them to the wall."

"Just out of curiosity," Reyes asked, "this place had to set you back a chunk of change. I have a nephew who's about your age — what, maybe twenty-five or so — and he's sitting on a decade's worth of student loan debt."

"I'll be twenty-seven next month," Zak explained. "My uncle loaned me the bulk of the money. Dave Klatter, he's a well-known cosmetic dentist. The rest of the money came from what I've scrimped and saved during active duty in the Guard."

"I've heard your uncle's commercials on Jack Plankinton's show," said Marks, a reference to a popular afternoon radio program. "Must be a high-end dentist."

"As my dad would say, my Uncle Dave's 'got the world by the balls.' He's never been married, had a vasectomy after graduating from dentistry school, owns a house on Pewaukee Lake, a condo on Marco Island in Florida, and has a car collection. The loan to me, he's joked, is like prematurely seeing his will in action."

"But if it's a loan," Singlaub asked, "you need to pay it back, right?"

"That's not how people with money roll," said Reyes. "Let me know if I'm right, Zak. Your uncle is forgiving $14,000 of the loan each year as a gift. So you're paying back just a fraction of what he loaned each year."

"You see," Zak replied, "there's reason he looks the part. My dad is also a finish carpenter, which really helped. He did most of the work in the pub at no cost, and built the bar from scratch."

CHAPTER SIX

"Okay, 2200 hours," Zak shouted. "It's a rap." Raul locked the pub's front and side doors, and followed Zak into the hallway. After setting the alarm, the two men scaled a flight of steps to the second floor apartment, where Xavier, Dwyer, and Ethan gathered around the kitchen table.

"How was business?" asked Ethan, who had Sundays off.

"We killed it during the football game," Zak replied. "After that, it was so-so." On the table was a twenty-by-twenty-three inch white, easel pad with a layout of the home near North 104th and West Lynx Road. "So this is the place. They use the rear door, which makes sense since it's out of view and blocked by the garage. The street looks more like an alley. What's on the other side of the scrub line?"

"Just green space," said Xavier. "Part of the Little Menomonee Parkway."

"It's great location, for them and us," Raul opined. "One street light, mid-block. A tree line along the property to the east. We could park the van there, get out, and approach the house from the garage. So what's the plan to get inside?"

Xavier pointed to the rear door. "Dudes order out for food all the time. The drivers take the food to the back door."

"Subterfuge," said Zak, as he sat back in a chair. "We'll get them to open the door under the guise of a food delivery."

"How much money are we talking about?" Ethan asked.

"If we hit it at the right time," Xavier explained, "about two hundred-and-fifty large. The third of the month is the best day to hit it. By that time, a lot of the money from SSI and other grants from the G made its way to the stash house." Xavier pointed to the pad with his right index finger. "The scratch is kept in the wall behind the stove, right here. Now, they got two Pits, but they lock them in the basement when food gets delivered or anyone stops in. The dogs, man, they're vicious as hell."

"The third of the month," Zak reasoned. "Okay, that gives us three weeks. Xavier and Dwyer, can you two do surveillance for the next two Saturdays from, let's say 2200 to 0200 Sunday morning?" Both men nodded affirmatively. "Good. Take the camera and get some good shots of the area, any vehicles, and, of course, people coming or going."

"Afterwards," Ethan added, "we'll be meeting here at 0230 next Sunday morning. We'll pile in the van, and train for the op at my uncle's warehouse. Plan on spending a good two hours there, so get some rest. I know Xavier and Dwyer work in the morning. I'll get you back here no later than 0530."

"Item number two," said Zak, "getting back at the prick bikers. I'd like to do it tomorrow morning, if we can get all hands on deck. Can everyone meet here in the garage by 0400?" Each man around the table nodded affirmatively.

"So what's the plan?" Dwyer asked.

"I've run it by Scrap. I'll fill in the rest of you tomorrow. Xavier, we'll need to swap the plates on your Durango again. Is that alright?"

"Yeah, that's cool, but I gotta be to work at eight."

"That shouldn't be a problem," Zak explained. "GPS shows the target leaves for work consistently at 0630. I've watched him arrive at work twice last week at 0650."

—

Raul quietly shut the side door of the building's one-car garage, slid a two-by-four into the door's fortified steel brackets, and joined the rest of the crew. Wearing purple surgical gloves, Zak removed an item wrapped in clear cellophane and placed the object on a workbench. "This, my friends, is half-kilo of cocaine."

Dwyer's eyes practically popped out of his head. "Where the hell did you get that?"

Zak smiled. "Let's just say I found it. I placed this sticky note on the coke." The other men looked at the small, yellow piece of paper, which read, *Take to Musty 1%er.* "The main thing is we cannot, I repeat, we cannot get caught with the coke. It'll be like a ten-year prison sentence if we do. Since I introduced the coke into the op, I'll assume the responsibility for holding it."

"So here's the plan," Ethan explained, as he placed a Slim Jim on the workbench. "We'll take the van to the target's home on South Burrell. We'll check out the area for a few minutes to make sure it's clear. Zak is going to get out of the van and wait in a gangway with the coke under his jacket. Once I get the truck's driver's door open, Zak will place the coke behind the front seat and put this .25 caliber pistol under the front seat."

"And the coke and pistol have been treated," Zak explained. "After Musty arrived at work last Tuesday, he was nice enough to spit out a piece of gum in the parking lot. I put on a pair of latex gloves, retrieved the gum, and used it to coat the plastic wrapper and the pistol's magazine with Musty's own DNA. Steve Singlaub gave me the idea after he said the police check for DNA in big dope cases."

"Now, once the coke is secured in Musty's truck," said Ethan, "we'll quietly shut the door. Once we're back in the van, Dwyer will drive around the block and park south of the target's truck. Then, we'll wait for Musty to leave for work. This is where Raul and Xavier come in."

Zak placed a black cell phone on the work bench. "This is an untraceable, never-been-used cell phone. You two will set up down the block. Once Musty leaves for work, follow him close enough to make all the lights. Raul, you'll call 9-1-1 and report that the occupant of the Ford truck cut you off, flipped you the finger, and then pointed a small pistol at you. Continue to follow Musty's truck at a distance until the police catch up to him. Then, turn off the cell phone and nonchalantly toss the phone into the Kinnickinnic River. We'll watch from a distance with binoculars. Then, if all goes well, we'll meet back here."

"Just checking," Ethan interjected. "Everyone's left their personal cell phones either in their cars or at home, right?" The four men nodded affirmatively. "Good. And everyone has the phones Zak provided, right." Again, each man nodded they had. "Okay, I've swapped out the plates on the van and on Xavier's car. If anyone does, for whatever reason, call us in, their plates will come back to someone else."

"One question, Scrap," Dwyer asked. "Are you sure you can get into the truck?"

"I worked in my dad's yard for six years," Ethan explained.

"There isn't a vehicle made I can't get into, especially an old truck without an alarm. Any other questions?" Ethan looked in each man in the eyes. "Seeing none. Let's hit it."

———

At 4:45 a.m., after scanning the neatly kept bungalow homes on South Burrell Street for twenty minutes, Ethan left the van with the Slim Jim tucked into the right sleeve of his jacket. Having concealed himself in a dark driveway just south of the Ford pickup, Zak continued to scan the area for potential onlookers. With the exception of Ethan, he saw nothing unusual. Due to a street light on the south side of the street, which the crew had failed to account for, Ethan approached the truck's passenger side, which was cloaked in darkness. Zak watched as his partner inserted the Slim Jim and vigorously moved the strip of metal. Ethan then pulled open the door, which made a loud, creaking sound. Ethan stood perfectly still. Zak poked his head out from the dark driveway. Seeing nothing unusual, he left and made his way to the pickup truck.

As Ethan stood lookout, Zak — his hands covered by surgical gloves — climbed on the front passenger's seat and removed the cocaine from a small plastic shopping bag. Bent over and kneeling on the passenger's seat, he placed the cocaine behind the driver's seat. As Zak removed the pistol from a second bag, a light in the living room of an upper-level duplex across the street came on. Startled, Zak quickly placed the pistol under the front seat and expeditiously closed the door, which, again, sent off a loud creaking sound. Suddenly, the upper-level porch light came on. A second later, Zak saw the door to the porch open. Zak and Ethan ducked down adjacent to the pickup's passenger side door. A man clad in sweatpants and a white t-shirt stepped onto the porch and lit a cigarette. "Shit," Ethan whispered. Occasionally taking drags from the cigarette, the man paced back and forth for five minutes, rugged the cigarette on the porch railing, and reentered the upper flat. The two men surveyed the area, and, after seeing no potential witnesses, made their way back to the van.

Once Ethan and Zak returned, Dwyer started the van, turned on the lights, and put the vehicle in drive. From the side view mirror, Dwyer spotted a black and white Milwaukee police cruiser turning left on Burrell Street from Morgan Avenue. "Get down," Dwyer advised, "it's the cops." The cruiser slowly made its way north on Burrell Street and stopped alongside the van.

An officer rolled down the passenger's side window of the police cruiser and leaned towards Dwyer. "Kind of quiet tonight," the officer shouted. "You heading to work?"

"Yeah," Dwyer smiled, "another day at the salt mine. Glad to see you in the neighborhood, officer."

"No problem," the young male officer replied. "When it's slow, I try to get the taxpayers the protection they deserve." The officer then rolled up the passenger side window, slowly continued north, and turned right on East Holt Avenue.

Dwyer wiped the perspiration from his forehead. "Shit, that was close."

"Just be glad he didn't have one of those license plate readers," said Ethan, "because the plates belong to a Ford Mustang."

"Damn it, Scrap," Dwyer shouted. "Couldn't you at least use plates that belong to a similar van?"

Ethan threw up his hands. "Hey, what can I say, beggars can't be choosey."

Dwyer then drove the van around the block, turned right from Morgan Avenue onto Burrell, and parked ten homes south of the Ford pickup. Zak punched the cell phone icon for Kramer, and Xavier answered the phone. "Okay," Zak muttered, "we had a couple close calls, but the package has been delivered. We're parked down the block with eyes on the target. Once we see it move, we'll give you a call."

"Just so you know," Xavier remarked, "we saw the popo up the block. Won't take them long to get here once we call."

"Yeah, we saw him, too," Zak replied, "too close for comfort. We'll give you a jingle if we see anything."

A little over an hour later, Musty unsuspectingly stepped from the side door of his home and went to his Ford pickup. He opened the driver's side door, but didn't notice that two pieces of paper he had placed on the front passenger's seat the prior evening had been displaced. The biker put the key in the ignition, fired up the engine, and turned on the lights.

Zak put in a call to Xavier. "Target is in vehicle ready to roll. Tell Raul to fire up the throwaway phone."

"Got it," said Xavier, as he spotted the pickup rolling north on Burrell Street. By the time the truck was traveling west on Holt Avenue, Xavier was just two car lengths behind. When Musty turned north onto South Chase Avenue, Raul called 9-1-1.

"City of Milwaukee emergency," said a female call taker, "how may I assist you."

"I just had some bearded dude in a pickup truck cut me off and point a pistol out the window at me," Raul replied.

"Do you have a location for the vehicle, sir?"

"Yeah, guy's going north on Chase Street just passing Piggly Wiggly. It's an old Ford truck. I'm following, but I don't want to get too close. He seems crazy."

In his rearview mirror, Xavier spotted a set of headlights quickly approaching. Soon, a black and white police cruiser shot passed him. "Ma'am," Raul told the call taker, "A police car just passed us and is now behind the truck. Tell him, he's right behind the truck."

"I will, sir, but please stay on the phone."

Suddenly, the red and blue lights of the police cruiser came to life. When Musty pulled the truck to the curb, Xavier took a right onto Euclid Avenue and left the area. Dwyer pulled the van to the curb a block south of the traffic stop and extinguished the van's lights. Looking through a pair of Vortex HD 15 x 50 binoculars, Ethan watched events unfold. A minute later, another police cruiser passed the van and stopped behind the first squad car. An officer directed Musty to step from the car, frisked him for weapons, and ordered him to the rear of the truck to speak with the second officer. The first officer then entered the interior of the truck. Less than a minute later, the officer quickly walked to the rear of the truck and put handcuffs on Musty. "Mission accomplished," Ethan told the occupants of the van. "Musty's in for a world of hurt."

"Couldn't happen to a nicer prick," said Dwyer. "Payback is a bitch."

Detective Garrett Marks entered a small, square interrogation room on the fourth floor of the Police Administration Building. Handcuffed to the wall was the enforcer for Nero's Ignitors Motorcycle Club. Marks unlocked the handcuffs. "Good morning, Mr. Romansky."

The biker's face cringed. "What's so fuckin' good about it?"

"A little surly today," said Marks. "Musty, this is Detective Gavin Fitzgerald."

"Aggghhh," Musty grunted.

"It's a pleasure to meet you, too, sir," said Fitzgerald. "But I understand why you're grouchy. You have some serious legal problems."

"Fuck you," Musty shouted. "I didn't do shit."

"You don't really have to do shit when you have cocaine," said Marks. "All you have to do is possess with intent to deliver."

A look of rage took over Musty's face. "I don't know anything about any drugs."

"Okay, well, it will be interesting to see how you explain away the 498 grams of coke in your truck," said Marks.

"That's bullshit. Your fellow cop must have planted that shit. I don't do coke, don't sell coke, and didn't have any coke."

Fitzgerald leaned forward. "Just so you know, Mr. Romansky, we're going to check the bag for DNA."

"Go for it," Musty shouted. "You won't find shit from me."

"Well, you know the drill, Musty," Marks explained. "Before we ask you any questions we're need to read your rights."

"Save it!" Musty shouted. "I ain't sayin' shit and I want my attorney, Mark Levinstein."

"Have it your way, Musty," Marks said. "We'll see you in court."

Seated at his desk, Assistant District Attorney Paul McGivens paged through the paperwork. "A member of Nero's Ignitors. I'm surprised the feds didn't take him."

"We ran up the ladder," Garrett Marks explained. "The U.S. Attorney's office isn't keen on the search. The feds won't touch anything they think is remotely shaky."

McGivens sat back in his chair. "The stop, based on *Navarette v. California*, seems good. The Supreme Court said an anonymous tip is good enough for an investigative stop. The citizen stating the driver of the truck pointed a gun at him is covered under the auspices of the Carroll doctrine. Have you located the person who called the police?"

"We've tried," Marks explained, "but the number can't be traced at this point. I have the 9-1-1 call on CD, if you care to listen to it. The caller, who sounds like a Hispanic male, said the driver pointed a gun at him. It was 6:23 in the morning. There was very little traffic on the road, and, of course, the officer found a gun in the car with the drugs."

"Is this Romansky a high-grade moron?" McGivens asked. "Who leaves a sticky note on a half-kilo of cocaine with their moniker on it?"

"Actually," Marks added, "I've always considered him to be real savvy. Then again, who knows? He might have been drunk or busy playing with some stripper's boobs. and simply forgot to remove the note."

McGivens plopped the paperwork on his desk. "I assume you're checking the packaging and the gun for DNA."

"Absolutely," said Marks, "but you know how that goes. Even if we push the envelope, it's going to be six to eight weeks to get anything back from the crime lab."

"Okay, I'll charge it," McGivens told the detective. "Even he pleads out, I'll drop the "while armed" enhancer. I'll need to throw Levinstein a bone. After all, he charges and an arm and leg."

CHAPTER SEVEN

Standing outside an enormous corrugated warehouse, Ethan depressed a series of buttons on a keypad. Having disarmed the alarm system, he used a key to open a heavy metal door, entered the dimly lit building, and flipped two light switches. "Damn, Scrap. Look at these big ass boats," Xavier shouted. "How much ching for these?"

"The one in front of us is an eighteen-year-old forty-one foot Maxum. It's probably worth a little over a hundred grand," said Ethan, as he pointed to a yacht in the corner. "Over there, that fifty-two foot Carver C52 Command Bridge: that could fetch about a nine hundred grand."

"The insurance on this place alone has got to be expensive," said Zak. "Your uncle must be doing something right."

"Storage is his business. Besides this building, he owns two thousand smaller units at eight locations in the metro area. He lives in Florida seven months out of the year. I take care of the building when he's gone for the winter. Follow me. From Xavier's sketch, I created a work up of the target."

After passing between two rows of high end yachts, a series of walls created with moveable partitions suddenly appeared. Dwyer opened a black gun case and removed the AR-15. Ethan opened a box and placed a Remington 870 shotgun, a revolver, and two semi-automatic pistols on a table. Zak carefully examined the firearms to ensued each was unloaded. Raul then double checked each weapon.

"All we're going to do this morning is focus on the entry to the house," Ethan explained. "What we know is this: one guy will answer the door and another will probably be in the living room. Once the door is open, we need to bum rush our way in, and take away the vision of the guy at the door."

"How are going to do that, Scrap?" asked a skeptical Raul.

Ethan removed a hand held canister from the box and placed it on the table. "This sixteen ounce cylinder of pepper spray can hit a target up to twenty-five feet. Once the door is open, we'll hit him right in the face with it. Then, he'll be unable to see. It's the second guy I'm worried about. When he hears the commotion, he'll respond to the rear door. If we can use his sidekick as a human shield, he'll hesitate long enough to be hit with a blast of pepper spray, too. We'll need the shotgun right there at the ready, just in case."

"What about the dogs?" Dwyer asked.

"If dude believes it's a food driver," Xavier explained, "the dogs will be put up somewhere, usually in the basement."

Ethan stood next to the mock-up front door. "Xavier, come over here role play the guy at the door." Xavier stood in the door's threshold. "Zak volunteered to walk up to the door disguised as a driver from Chicken Wings Unlimited." Ethan reach into a second cardboard box. He removed a Chicken Wings Unlimited t-shirt and ball cap. "I got this stuff online. Even better, one of my roommates in college got drunk one night and tore off a Chicken Wings Unlimited car topper, which I've hung on to."

"The plan sounds cool," Xavier said, "but how we goin' to get the dudes to order wings?"

"They're not," Zak explained. "I'll bring the chicken to the door. It may take a little coaxing, but hopefully the guy will either believe his partner ordered the chicken or think someone else mistakenly sent the food to the wrong address. It doesn't really matter, as long as he opens the door. After that, it's about the element of surprise."

Xavier chuckled. "Those brothers up in there ain't never going to suspect a straight up white dude, like Zak."

"Now Xavier," Zak added, "you're going to be just to my right at the door. After spraying the guy, you'll bark any necessary orders to them. We want these dope dealers to believe they're being robbed by a crew from the hood. We'll be wearing balaclavas with goggles to protect our eyes from the pepper spray. If things go well, they'll never get a glimpse of what we look like."

For the better part of an hour, the five men practiced the entry. Zak pretended to knock at the door. Crouched down to his right, Xavier sprang into action and greeted the first man with a burst of pepper spray. Zak then grabbed the man from behind. Dwyer quickly entered with a shotgun loaded with double O buckshot. When the second man appeared in the kitchen, Xavier was prepared to pepper spray him. Then, Ethan and Raul entered to secure the two men with flexi-cuffs.

———

At twenty minutes after midnight, off-duty detectives Steve Singlaub, Garrett Marks, and Gavin Fitzgerald walked through the front door and made a beeline for the few open seats at the bar. Ethan grabbed three coasters and approached the thirsty customers. "Gentlemen, what will it be tonight?"

"We'll have a pitcher of Lennie's Octoberfest," said Marks.

"This guy really did this place justice," Fitzgerald told his colleagues. "The woodwork and the bar look great."

"His old man is a finish carpenter," said Singlaub.

Ethan returned with a glass pitcher of cold beer and three glasses. "Are you guys running a tab?"

"Yeah," Marks replied, "I'm buying tonight."

Exiting the kitchen, Zak spotted the detectives seated at the bar and went to greet them. "What's going on, fellas?"

"We're celebrating tonight," said Marks. "And you should be happy, too. We just took down Musty from Nero's Ignitors — the knucklehead that cut you off on K.K."

"For what?" Zak asked.

"A big time dope case," Marks answered. "And he whined like as stuck pig, even claimed one of our coppers planted the dope in his truck."

Zak smiled and shook Marks' hand. "Good work! Ethan, next pitcher is on the house for these guys."

"Yeah," Singlaub grinned, "we got him good this time. With that prior felony conviction, Musty's probably looking at least fifteen years."

"Holy shit," Zak added, "that's some serious time."

"We're hoping it's enough to get him to roll on the club," said Marks. "Those N.I. assholes are good for at least three open homicides."

Zak shook his head in disbelief. "When will people learn that crime doesn't pay?" Suddenly, the side door opened, Mandy entered, and took a seat at an open stool at the far end of the bar. Zak excused himself and made his way to Mandy.

"Wow," Marks said between sips of beer, "now that young lady is well endowed."

While his colleague ogled the woman at the end of the bar, Fitzgerald's memory kicked in. Zak, it seemed, matched the description of the white male who had recovered the discarded duffel bag tossed from the window of the fleeing Audi months earlier. "Just curious," Fitzgerald mused, "your friend, Zak, about how old do you think he is."

"He's going to be twenty-seven next month," Singlaub replied. "My guess is there's gonna be one hell of a party here."

Fitzgerald rubbed his thumb and index finger on his chin. "I'm just wondering: where does a young guy like Zak get the money to open a spot like this?"

"His uncle is a big-time cosmetic dentist," said Marks. "He advertises on Jack Plankinton's show. You've heard the ads, 'For teeth whiter than the purest snow, Klatter Dentistry is the place to go.' His uncle loaned him the money. What's got your undies in bundie, Gavin?"

"A few months ago," Fitzgerald explained, "a source reported a white male, fitting Zak's description, was walking on 55th Street when a green duffle bag from a drug rip was tossed out the window. I spent some time down in this area checking the video from businesses on North Avenue looking for the elusive white male, but this place hadn't been opened yet."

"Zak is clean as a whistle," Singlaub insisted. "When my brother told me about The Fallen, I checked him out. One speeding ticket, which proves he's human. And, by the looks of his lady friend over there, the man likes fast cars and fast women. If that's a crime, well, fifty percent of the male population would be in jail."

Lying in the prone position, Xavier's right index finger slowly squeezed the trigger until the loud boom surprised him. When the range master gave the "all clear" signal, five other shooters placed their weapons on the ground and walked forty yards down range. Xavier retrieved his target, returned to the shooting platform, and showed the human silhouette to Ethan. "That's some damn good shootin', Xavier. A group the size of a baseball."

"Yeah," Xavier laughed, "I'm a little rusty. When I was in the Marines, I used to group them smaller than this at a hundred yards."

"It's a good thing," Ethan explained, "that everyone on this crew is a good shot. I took Raul and Dwyer to an indoor range last week. Both were lights out with the pistols. And you're good with the shotgun, right?"

Xavier slapped Ethan on the back. "Come on, Scrap. I could load, fire, and hit a target with a pump action in the dark of the night, man. When I was a kid, my mama had a shotgun up in our house. Knew that thing inside, outside by the time I was ten."

"But you know how that goes," Ethan replied. "Things are different under stress. I'm not worried about you and Zak. You've both been in combat. It's Dwyer and Raul. Sure, they're dead-eye shooters at an indoor range, but if things go to shit, we can only hope they can hit what they're shooting at under duress. Have you heard anything more from your cousin about the target?"

"He was there two nights ago," Xavier replied. "They're still stashin' the scratch in the wall behind the stove. The same two dudes — the ones who let their guards down — should be at the place when we hit it. My cuz said food was delivered twice while he was there last week. One time, they put the dogs in the basement, another time in a bedroom. The drivers were told to take the delivers to the back door."

Ethan's eyes looked toward the sky. "Good. We've drilled this thing for ten hours, trained with our equipment, have good Intel, and solid surveillance photos. Any loose-ends you can think of?"

Xavier thought for a moment. "Nothin' I can think of. Time to knock this thing out."

"It's a wrap," Zak shouted, as the last of the pub's customers — a well-dressed middle-age couple — exited the front entrance at five minutes after nine. It had been a quiet Sunday night on the third day of the month. After locking the front and side doors, Zak and Raul stepped into an adjacent hallway, made sure the alarm was set, and scaled a flight on steps, where Dwyer, Ethan, and Xavier nervously gathered around the kitchen table inside the apartment. Zak looked directly into each man's eyes. "Game on."

"We're ready to roll," Ethan replied. "The van's backed into the garage. I put a set of bogus plates on the van and Xavier's ride."

"Listen up," Zak shouted, in a serious tone of voice. "You know the drill. We've gone over it a dozen times. I'll drive Xavier's ride to the church lot near 99th and Good Hope and put the Chicken Wings Unlimited topper on. The van will take a different route, meet up with me at the church, and follow me to the target. Once we hit the place, strip yourselves of all garb, clear your weapons, account for every round of ammo, and place all the equipment in your duty bags. I'll take Route A back. The van will take Route B. These routes were selected to minimize exposure to street level surveillance cameras. There is a down side: it will take us longer to distance ourselves from the area."

"The only cell phones or other devices you should be carrying are those Zak issued," Ethan advised. "And all of your personal cell phone are at home and on, correct?" Each man nodded affirmatively. "If the police do somehow suspect us, the personal cell phones will show each of us was home at the time of the op."

"From what we've been told," Zak told the crew, "the police do not have ShotSpotter censors in the area."

"What's that?" Xavier asked.

"ShotSpotter is a network that triangulates gunshots in a matter of seconds," Zak explained. "The Com Center receives a notification and cops are sent to the precise area. The point being, if shots are fired during this op, we'll have some extra time to get out of there."

"Does anyone have any other questions?" Ethan looked at

each man at the table. "Alright then. Let's head down to the garage and, with the exception of Zak, garb up."

In the garage, four large duty bags, each bearing a crew members initials, rested on the floor. Each contained a dark jump suit, dark gloves, a black balaclava mask, ski goggles, a ballistic vest, a firearm, and loaded magazines. Xavier's bag also contained the large canister of pepper spray and four sets of flexi cuffs. "Before you touch anything," Zak told the crew, "glove up. I personally loaded each of these magazines with gloves on. If, God forbid, rounds are fired, the shell casings expended will be fingerprint and DNA free." Clad in a Wings Unlimited t-shirt and ball cap, Zak looked on as the four other men checked each other's gear.

When Ethan opened the rear door of the van, Xavier, Dwyer, and Raul climbed inside. The three men took seats on carpeted benches mounted to the side walls. Two folded duffel bags rested on the behind the front driver's seat, which, if things went as planned, would house the stolen cash. Ethan climbed into the front driver's seat, drove the van from the garage, and depressed a button that closed the overhead door.

As Zak drove west to the freeway, the van traveled to the met spot via Appleton Avenue. Ethan, with the brim of his ball cap and the van's sun visor pulled down, was confident the bogus license plates would make it virtually impossible for street level surveillance cameras to identify the owner of the vehicle or the driver. After all, the van was registered to one of his uncle's customers, and supposedly stowed away at a secure warehouse.

Hyper-paranoid, the three men in the back of the van stared through the vehicle's rear tinted windows on the lookout for police vehicles. At 2200 hours on a Sunday night, the van hardly stood out on a street traversed by cars sporting $5,000 rims. Ethan exited Appleton Avenue at 107th Street. The van then traveled north to Good Hope Road. Within a matter of minutes, Ethan turned into the church parking lot, and pulled long side the Dodge Durango. Zak stepped outside, walked to the van, and slide open the rear passenger's side door. "Okay, follow me to the target. Once you guys are in position, I'll circle the block, park in the rear driveway, and approached the rear door. I'll checkout the house before knocking. If I thrust my fist in the air, the op is off. If I remove my ball cap, the op is a go. Good luck. May the good Lord be with us."

In an effort to avoid as many street level surveillance cameras as possible, the crew's two vehicles drove south on 99th Street, took the backroads to Little Menomonee Parkway, and turned right onto Mill Road. A few minutes passed before the van was parked just east of the target, but just west of a tall scrub line that seemingly concealed the van from a residence to the east. Ethan examined the stash house with a pair of high-power binoculars, but saw nothing unusual. A minute later, Zak pulled the red Durango into the driveway, quietly exited with an order of chicken fried in The Fallen's kitchen, and approached the rear door. Peering through a crack between a pulled down shade and the wooden interior door frame, he caught a glimpse of the kitchen.

Looking on from the van, Ethan saw Zak removed his ball cap. "Alright," Ethan told the rest of the crew, "let's move out. Being stealthy is the key. Move quietly, follow the south end of the garage to the home. Then, line up in order to the north of the rear door."

Xavier slowly pulled the van's side door open. Each man, seeking to make as little noise as possible, slowly filed out. Being the last man out of the van, Ethan slowly closed the sliding door, but did not shut it tight. The men in black jump suits quickly made their way to the side of the home. With the large pepper stray canister in his right hand, Xavier gave Zak a thumbs up.

With the order of chicken in his hands, Zak rang the doorbell and the dogs began to bark. Ten seconds later, the rear porch light came to on, and a young black man, wearing a wool skull cap, pulled back the right side of the blind. "Delivery," Zak sternly shouted. "I've got your wings."

The man disappeared for a moment. Fifteen seconds later, he returned to the door. "We didn't order up no chicken. You got the wrong house."

Zak lifted a piece of paper stapled to the orders white packaging. "It's the right address," said Zak, thinking on his feet. "The order was sent here by Junior. It was paid for with a debit card." Through a crack in the blind, Zak saw a man escort two Pitbull dogs into a room and close the door. The man returned to the door. Zak heard the man manipulate the interior dead bolt lock and stepped back a few feet. When the door swung open, the would-be customer took a half-step outside before Xavier hit him with a burst of pepper spray.

"Ahhhh, what the fuck!" the man shouted. As Zak stepped away from the door, Xavier turned the man around from behind and forced him into the kitchen. Armed with the shotgun, Dwyer peered just over the human shield's right shoulder. A man quickly emerged from the living room toting a large revolver. With his colleague in the line of fire, the second man hesitated just long enough to get hit with a burst of pepper spray.

"Mother fuck!" the man screamed. Xavier then shouted, "Get your asses down on the floor!" Dwyer quickly moved towards the second man and, fearing he may begin to randomly fire, slammed the shotgun's wooden stock into the left side of the coughing man's head. After securing the first man's hands, Xavier tossed a second pair of flexi cuffs to Dwyer, who placed them on the now semi-conscious second man's hands.

Ethan and Raul quickly moved in and, with the exception of the bedroom where the dogs were secured, cleared the rest of the house. Finding no other persons inside, Xavier and Dwyer pulled their two victims into the living room. "Y'all better shut the fuck up," Xavier shouted, "or I'll put a bullet in your fuckin' heads!" With Xavier covering the two men, Dwyer stood lookout near the rear door. Inside the bedroom, the two dogs barked and clawed at the wooded door.

As Raul and Ethan pulled the stove from the wall, Zak entered the living room and went into acting mode. "Please don't kill me!" Zak yelled. "I'm just a college student delivering chicken to pay tuition. I've got nothing to do with this." Through the gap in his mask, Zak saw Xavier crack a smile.

"Shut the fuck up, punk ass!" Xavier shouted to Zak. "I got no problems cappin' your Lily white ass."

With the stove pulled from the wall, Ethan used a screw driver to pry open the drywall cover. Peering inside the two by four foot cubbyhole with a LED flashlight, Ethan saw piles of cash as high as the eye could see. He frantically began handing the contents to Raul, who quickly stuffed the cash in the duffel bags. Ten minutes later, the cubbyhole was empty. Ethan replaced the dry wall cover and pushed the stove back against the wall. Raul walked into the living room and gave Xavier and Zak the sign to leave.

"Mr. Delivery Driver," Xavier screamed. "Your ass better stay in his room and count to a hundred before you leave. If you call the cops, I'll hunt you down making deliveries and you'll be a dead man."

"Please, please, don't kill me," Zak screamed. "I'll do whatever you say."

With the crew reassembled in the kitchen, Dwyer scanned the area from the rear door, gave a thumbs up sign, and the five men quietly filed from the house. Zak, who was the last to leave, depressed a lock in the door's handle and shut the door behind him.

Realizing the consequences of losing the money, the two men lying on the living room floor began to panic. "Hey, white boy," shouted one of the men, believing the delivery driver was still in the living room. "Get these things off us before you leave, man, and I'll give you a thousand dollars." To their chagrin, the delivery driver never answered.

Residing in a small, two-story home to the east of the target, seventy-one-year-old Rosemary Hackbarth thought she had heard strange noises coming from outside her partially opened second-story bedroom window. Not as nimble as she once was, the elderly woman pulled back a quilt, slowly rolled out of bed, and looked out the window to the west. With her glasses resting on a nearby nightstand, Hackbarth saw what appeared to be two men dressed in all black enter a van, as an SUV backed out of the driveway.

"George," Rosemary said to her sleeping seventy-seven-year-old husband, "Something's going on next door."

"Stop being so nosey. I just fell asleep."

"Something strange is going on, George."

"How can you tell without your glasses," the elderly man mumbled. "You're as blind a bat without them."

Rosemary admonished her husband. "Stop being so damn stubborn. Something happened over there. I'm going to call the police."

"Oh, sure, call the police," George responded. "That ought to make us real popular with our neighbors, who are quiet enough and keep to themselves."

Rosemary retrieved her glasses and picked up a receiver for a landline telephone. "Don't call the police. I'll get my shoes on and check on it myself."

Having severed two tours in Vietnam, George Hackbarth didn't get excited about much, even the gun shots he occasionally heard from a nearby troubled neighborhood. Clad in a light jacket and pajama pants, he slipped on his glasses, exited the rear door, and headed west on Lynx Road. The one operable street light illuminated the area fairly well. After climbing four wooden steps to his neighbor's rear door, George peered through the small crack between the shade and the window frame. A chill ran down his spine when he spotted a silver revolver and blood on the kitchen floor. *Oh my God*, he thought, *for the first time in her life, Rosemary's suspicions were right.*

———

Ethan pulled the van into the garage attached to the rear of The Fallen. When the overhead door closed, the four occupants emerged from the side door and met Zak, who had arrived minutes earlier. Each member of the entry team placed their duty bags on the floor. Ethan reached into each bad, retrieved the firearms, and unloaded each weapon. He then returned the original license plates to the van and Xavier's Durango, which was parked outside.

With the gear back in the van, Ethan and Raul retrieved the two duffel bags then followed the others upstairs to Zak's apartment. The vast majority of the cash had already been bundled in thousand dollars stacks. It took an hour-and-half to sort and count the loose bills. Zak added the bundles together on a plastic calculator. Then, he announced the total: $325,725.

"Before we divvy this up," Zak noted, "we have some expenses I would like to cover. I've laid out $5,000 in cash for the botched AR buy, the actual AR buy, ammo, magazines, and gear. Scrap's contribution for the guns, ammo, range time, vests and gas also $2,000. Is everyone good with the ten large of reimbursements before we divide the spoils?" Dwyer, Raul, and Xavier raised no objections. Zak grabbed seven stacks of money and passed two stacks to Ethan.

"Would it be cool to put the $725 into a beer and food fund at the bar?" Dwyer asked. "That should cover our tabs when we stop in for a while."

"Any objections," Zak asked. "Seeing none, that leaves $315,000 minus $31,500 for Xavier's cousin."

"Why give his cousin that much?" Raul asked. "He doesn't know the total amount."

"Look," Zak explained, "Xavier's cousin hangs at the house. He may hear how much was actually lost in the robbery. It's also not going to take him long to realize Xavier isn't working for the feds. The last thing we need is a snitch. As long as he is getting his share of proceeds, he'll fall in line and soon realize he's an accomplice. What's he going to do, rat out himself?"

"Not trying to be disrespectful," Dwyer added, "but how do we know Xavier will give his cousin the money?"

Xavier didn't miss a beat. "I'll get a picture of him with the money and show it to y 'all."

"Alright," Ethan interjected, "so were good with the percentage for Xavier's cousin. That leaves us $56,700 each."

Zak and Ethan then counted, recounted, and divided the piles of cash for each participant. Before leaving, Zak issued each member of the crew a warning. "Don't flash the money around. Refrain from making more than one purchase over a grand a month. Scrap and Raul, if you want some of the cash washed through the pub, leave it behind. Raul and Ethan handed half of their stacks to Zak.

"The van might be hot, so I'll be spending the night," Ethan told the others. "Zak and I will walk you to your cars armed to the teeth, but, after that, you're on your own. We'll debrief here next Sunday night at 2300 hours. Until then, lay low and don't say shit about this to anyone — Xavier and his cousin being the exception."

Felix Montes, the officer sent to investigate what he believed to be a home invasion armed robbery, was seated in the rear of Detective Gavin Fitzgerald's unmarked squad car. "So tell me what you've got so far?" Fitzgerald asked.

"At about 11:30 p.m.," Montes began, glancing down at a brown memo book, "an elderly woman in the house just to the east — a Rosemary Hackbarth — heard strange noises coming from the victim residence. She didn't have her glasses on, so her vision was somewhat blurred. She claims to have observed two men, of an unknown age, race, and height, entering a dark colored conversion van through the side door. She thinks one of the men had a long gun. Rosemary woke up her seventy-seven year-old husband. After some back-and-forth, she convinced her husband, George, to check on the welfare of their neighbors. When George got to the neighbor's rear door, he looked between a crack in the shade and the door frame, and saw a silver revolver and blood on the kitchen floor. He immediately returned home and called 9-1-1.

"After I arrived, I confirmed the caller's observations by looking through the same window. Two minutes later, the second squad arrived. We pounded at the door, and heard individuals inside screaming and dogs barking. I then forced entry by kicking in the door. We found two black males, their hands bound with flexi cuffs, in the living room. Both men had been peppered sprayed. One of the men had good sized welt on the side of his head."

"Who are the men inside the house?" Fitzgerald asked.

"The first male, the one with the welt, is Infiniti T. Ivey, age twenty-nine. He's a two time convicted felon for possession with intent to deliver. He claims to reside here. The second man is Maurice Bruce, age twenty-two, who gave an address as 5640 N. 43rd Street. He has an outstanding warrant for battery. Ivey is at Froedtert Hospital with a copper."

"Well," Fitzgerald asked, "what does Bruce have to say?"

Montes laughed. "He said he didn't see shit. When I asked him who pepper sprayed and bound him, his response was, 'Your mama.'"

"Hum, a real asshole," Fitzgerald mumbled. "I know Ivey. He's one of Trey Downing's drug runners. This could be a stash house. Trey's group is at war with the 4-5 Mob. Word on the street has it the 4-5's ripped one of Trey's guys a few months ago for a hundred grand. I'm surprised either of these mopes were dumb enough to open the door, which leads me to believe it had to be someone they knew. Who's processing the scene inside?"

"That'd Richards, from the ID Section," Montes replied, "and two violent crimes detectives."

"Since they caught the case," Fitzgerald told the officer, "tell them I'll respond to the hospital. It's been a while since I spoke with Ivey, but we go back a ways."

Unlike so many of the anti-social characters involved in the vice underground, Infiniti Ivey was personable, smart, and charismatic. If he hadn't been co-opted by the narco-gang element, Ivey, Fitzgerald believed, would have made an excellent politician. During his contacts with the police, Ivey never burned bridges. A decade-a-half earlier, Fitzgerald recalled his first contact with Ivey —a foot chase near 37th and W. Hampton, where the young man sold dime bags of crack cocaine on the street for the Farwell brothers. Now, it seemed, Ivey had paid his dues and clawed his way through the ranks of Trey Downing's organization.

After arriving at Froedtert Hospital, Fitzgerald walked through a large ambulance bay, entered the complex through a set of sliding doors, and walked down a bright hall with a white tiled floor. Entering the emergency room, he approached a nurse's station. "Detective Fitzgerald from Milwaukee. I'm looking for Infiniti Ivey, here with a head injury."

A nurse in her early thirties glanced at a white board. "He's in room twelve, off to the right."

After thanking the nurse, the detective walked thirty feet, peered into room twelve, and spotted a young, female officer keeping tabs on the alleged victim. "What up, old school?" Ivey shouted after Fitzgerald entered the room. "I haven't seen you in a while, man. Thought you retired, playin' some golf, or layin' on a beach somewhere."

Fitzgerald turned to the female officer. "Unless you have anything for me, I can take if from here."

"Nothing," the officer replied. "Mr. Ivey has talked about everything under the Sun, except of the details of tonight's incident." The officer collected her jacket, said goodbye to the detective, and left the room.

"So you thought I retired," said Fitzgerald. "I guess that means one of two things: either I'm out of the mix or you're moving up the ladder and keeping a low profile."

"Come on, detective, you know it ain't like that. But you gotta be retiring soon, dog. What's left of your hair is grandpa gray. How much longer you got left, man?"

Fitzgerald glanced at his watch. "Six months, twelve days, one hour and thirty-six minutes. But, hey, who's counting."

Ivey laughed. "It's that bad, hah. Seems like all y'all cashin' it in as soon as you can. I haven't seen any of the dudes from the old G squad in a long time. You're like the last man standing."

"I'm the ass end of the baby boom generation of cops," Fitzgerald added, "but, unlike a lot of crew on the old gang squad, I didn't come on the job until I was twenty-nine. Can't wait to pull the pin, though."

"Yeah, I've seen your guy from union on TV bitchin' about the chief."

"The chief is part of it, no doubt about that." Fitzgerald added. "The other part is generational. The standards around here have really fallen. Some of these young coppers look like they've just rolled out of bed and came to work."

"Man, I hear what you're sayin'. I saw a dude in one of y'all's uniforms a few days ago with long-ass dreads dyed gold. Looked like he just got out of prison."

Fitzgerald laughed. "Yeah, it's time to move on and make room for the millennial generation. Besides catching up on old times, you know why I'm here right?"

"Yeah, the shit at the house," Ivey frowned. "Tell me, old school, what do you think happened?"

The detective cut to the chase. "I think you got ganked by the 4-5 Mob."

"Well, as far as that goes," Ivey carefully said, "I slipped on some dog dukey and smacked my head on the floor."

Fitzgerald laughed "Sure, and you fell into a pool pepper spray and rolled into some flexi cuffs, too, right? Look, I get it. That's your official version. It's the unofficial version — how much money was stolen and who was in-charge of the stash — that's going to be the real problem. I don't see Trey letting his money walk without someone paying a price."

Ivey sighed. "Yeah, things could get complicated, man...real complicated."

"Here's the deal, Infiniti: I've only got a few months left on this project. On the way out the door, I'm trying to put a case on the 4-5 Mob. If you jump ship now and came over to my side, I might be able to get you witness relocation."

Ivey thought for a minute. "I dunno, man. My babies' mamas be here. Leaving Milwaukee, that's some heavy shit."

"Well, it's better than being six feet under. You're never going to see your babies' mamas that way. Here's my card. I'm at Milwaukee HIDTA now. Trey's going to be looking for you, so think it over."

Fitzgerald turned and walked for the door. "Hey, old school," said Ivey, "thanks for the number."

CHAPTER EIGHT

"All rise," shouted a middle-age white bailiff, whose black-and-gray goatee seemingly covered half of his oval face. "Milwaukee County Circuit Court Branch Sixteen is now in session. The Honorable Theresa M. Luterbach presiding. Your silence is commanded. Please be seated." Dressed in a black robe, the fit judge in her late thirties took a seat behind the bench. The bailiff reached for a file and called the first case. "State of Wisconsin versus Derrick Romansky: possession with intent to deliver while armed, felon in possession of a firearm."

"Appearances please," asked the judge.

"Assistant District Attorney Paul McGivens for the state."

"Mark Levinstein appearing on behalf of Mr. Romansky."

The judge looked to the defense table. "The case is here today for arraignment. Mr. Levinstein, how does your client plead?"

"Not guilty."

"With that plea," said the judge, "let's set a date for a status conference."

"January 9th at 1:30," the court clerk shouted.

"That works for me," Levinstein shouted.

"Mr. McGivens?" the judge asked.

"That date is fine with the state. At this time, I am providing the defendant with thirty-three pages of discovery."

"Mr. Levinstein," said the judge, "it's my understanding you're requesting a bail modification."

"I am, your honor. At the preliminary hearing, the magistrate set bail at one million dollars, which is extremely excessive when considering the facts of this case and my client's background. Mr. Romansky has been resident of Milwaukee County his entire life. He owns a home, and has been employed by the same company for twelve years. The defense would ask that bail be reduced to $50,000. Because of high bail, Mr. Romansky has been in custody since his arrest five weeks ago. He's used all of his vacation and flex time. If he doesn't return to work soon, he'll likely lose his job."

"Mr. McGivens," asked the judge, "what is the state's positon on bail?"

"The defendant is a convicted felon, who, as alleged in the criminal complaint, was in possession of over a pound of cocaine and a firearm. He is also a member of Nero's Ignitors Motorcycle Club — a group with a history of violence and one that maintains chapters throughout the United States, Canada, Europe, and Russia. With a lengthy prison sentence a distinct possibility, the state sees the defendant as a flight risk."

"This isn't homicide or sexual assault case," the judge mused. "Although the allegations are serious, Mr. Romansky, based on the facts alleged in the criminal complaint, does not appear to be a threat to a particular party in the community. And, unlike so many of our defendants, he is gainfully employed. I'll modify bail to $200,000."

Levinstein whispered into his client's ear. "Can you come up with the cash?"

"Yeah," Musty mumbled, "if I put up my house up as collateral."

"Good. Once you're released, call my office and make an appointment to see me. I'll have copies of discovery ready for you."

———

Xavier had established a rule to live by: never conduct business in "the hood" after 11 a.m. At about that time, drug dealers, thieves, fiends, and frauds rolled out of bed and wandered about Milwaukee's north side. Mookie, on the other hand, wasn't a fan of Xavier's 9 a.m. Saturday morning meet. The end result was Xavier pounding on his cousin's first-floor bedroom window. Dressed in white t-shirt and long underwear, Mookie pushed himself out of bed, pulled back a blind, and saw Xavier pointing towards the front door. Groggy, he stumbled into the living room barefoot, undid the death bolt lock, opened the door, and saw Xavier holding a white clothes basket.

"Come on, cuz," a Mookie mumbled, "you got my sorry ass out of bed this early so you could come over and do clothes. Seriously, man, it's Saturday morning."

"Chill out, Mookie, and close the damn door."

"Dude," Mookie mumbled, as he disappeared into the sparsely furnished kitchen. "I need some coffee."

Xavier took a seat on a tattered couch and placed the clothes basket between his feet. A minute later, Mookie emerged from the kitchen with two cups of coffee, and handed one to Xavier.

"What's so damn important?" Mookie asked.

"I'm just takin' care of business before the fools wake up."

"Business? What you talkin' about?"

Xavier reached into the laundry basket, retrieved a large brown paper bag concealed under a pile of dirty clothes, and heaved the sack at his cousin. "It's payday, bro!"

When Mookie opened the bag the groggy, hungover feeling that had hold of him momentarily abated. "Holy shit, dog, the feds musta hit it!"

"Sure did. Scooped up over three hundred big ones. That's $31,800 for you. Don't be flashin' it around those holes at the club."

Mookie shrugged his shoulders and smiled. "You know it ain't like that, cuz. Look at the crib. I need some furniture to move some girls around on."

"You can do what you want with it, man. It's all yours, tax free. Just glad you got my six so I can work off this case. Mookie, man, your good fortune calls for a little celebration. What you got to toast with?"

"I dunno if I'm up to that," Mookie frowned. "I'm still lit from last night."

"Come on, cuz," Xavier barked. "I did you right. Least you could is throw back a couple with me."

Mookie walked into the kitchen. Thirty seconds later, he returned with two plastic cups and a bottle of Johnny Walker Red. He poured an ounce-and-a-half of whiskey in both cups and passed one to his guest.

Xavier raised his glass to toast. "To more money!"

Two shots later, and already intoxicated Mookie lit a Phillie blunt laced with marijuana. "Sure you don't want a hit?"

"Naw, I'm good with the whiskey. Man, look at all that money. Think you'll ever be sittin' in front of stacks this big again?"

Mookie set the blunt in an ashtray and grabbed as many of the thousand dollar stacks as he could in each hand. "I dunno, but damn, this sure feels good!"

Xavier reached for his iPhone. "Raise those stacks in the air. Say 'more money!'" Mookie did as he was told and Xavier snapped a photo.

Twenty minutes later, the contents of Mookie's stomach began to swirl. "I ain't feelin' so good." He stood up, quickly went to the bathroom, and vomited in the commode. A few minutes later, he staggered out of the bathroom. "Sorry, cuz. I'm gonna get my ass back to bed."

"Cool," Xavier replied, "I'll hit it then. We'll kick it sometime this week." Xavier opened the door, glanced at his phone, which read 9:50, and made a beeline to the Durango before "the fools" woke up.

———

His hands and feet duct-taped to a large, wooden chair, Maurice "Mo Mo" Bruce stared around a dank former strip club in the 4700 block of Hopkins Street. Although he had been shot in the abdomen during a drug deal gone-bad at age seventeen, he had never contemplated death, until now. For the past half hour, four heavily armed men — the same group that had stuffed him inside a cargo van at gun point — formed a semi-circle in front of him. Bruce heard a door behind him open. Soon, all six-foot-seven of Trey Downing, dressed in a black Nike athletic outfit, emerged and stopped in front of him.

"You got one fuckin' chance," said Downing in a low, menacing voice, "to tell us what we need to know. You're just one lie from being a dead man." Downing reached to the rear waistband of his pants, produced a chrome .357 revolver, and pointed the gun inches from Bruce's face. "I want the names of every son of a bitch that ever came up into that house when you was there."

Three feet behind Downing, a man dressed in all black removed a small notepad and pen from a jacket pocket.

"Let me see," said a trembling Bruce, "there was Juju and J.T."

"Damn it!" Downing shouted. "Stop bullshitting me. They're members of our crew, so we know they'd been up in there. I'm talkin' about motherfuckers that shouldn't been up in there."

"Trey, man," Bruce mumbled, "it ain't like that. I mean…"

Downing reached for a sledge hammer and dropped the object Bruce's left foot. "Ahhhhhhhhhh!" the bound man screamed.

"Quit bullshittin' me, Mo Mo!"

"Alright, man," Bruce mumbled, as he cringed in pain. "Finny [Infiniti Ivey] let a few dudes kick it there."

"And who these dudes be?" Downing asked.

"Lil Dre, Peabody, and Mookie."

An irate Downing stared at Bruce. "What were those three doing up in there?"

"Ah, ah, just kickin' it," Bruce stuttered. "Playin' video games. We didn't say shit to them."

"You dumb fucks!" Downing shouted. "I told y'all not to let anybody up in that house!"

"I don't know the dudes, man." Bruce quickly replied. "Finny let them in."

Downing turned to the men behind him. "Anyone know these names?"

"Peabody is that light-skinned dude with funky lookin' round ass glasses," the man taking notes said. "He lives up over on thirty-fifth by Villard."

"Anything on the other two?" Downing shouted. None of the men answered.

Downing pointed the gun inches from Bruce's nose. "I should cap your ass right now, but we need to find out who these motherfuckers is. You got two days to find Finny. If you don't, your fucked up foot won't be hurtin' anymore cuz your ass will be dead."

The breeze from a half-open bedroom window helped Zak descend into a deep sleep. Minutes later, his mind carried him to a rugged green field just outside the village of Khanabad, Afghanistan. Lying in the prone positon, he concealed his heavily camouflaged body between two berms of green brush, while conducting surveillance of a dilapidated farm house one hundred meters to the east with a pair of Steiner 8x30 binoculars. Suddenly, an earpiece crackled to life. "Romeo One," said a fellow solider overlooking the area from a nearby hill, "activity at your seven." Zak's eyes moved as far to the left as they could without moving his head, but his peripheral vision was unable to detect any movement. Then, after a foot was thrust onto his neck, two Afghani men began screaming in Dari. One man sunk a foot into their captive's left side. Zak's head turned slightly to the right. Out of the corner of his eye, he spotted a stainless steel machete plunging towards his neck. "Noooooooooooooooooooooooooooo!"

Covered in perspiration, Zak's upper body sprang upright in bed. Shaken by the scream, Mandy put her right arm around Zak. "What happened? What's going on? Are you okay?"

Zak looked at a digital alarm clock adjacent to the bed, which read 4:12. "Yeah," he muttered as he rubbed his eyes, "just one hell of a bad dream. I was back in Afghanistan dug in on a surveillance."

"Everything's alright, Zak. Remember what Doc Moreau said. Flashbacks can be a form of self-preservation."

"I remember," Zak replied, "but I've never had flashbacks before. The dream was surreal."

Mandy ran her left hand though Zak's thick brown hair. "It could be the business, you know, trying to make it, trying to persevere. Some of the things we experience can trigger thoughts from theater, especially for people like you, who got off living on the edge."

"Well, I'm wide awake now. I'm going to grab a glass of water." After getting up from bed, he put on a robe, made his way to the kitchen, and poured a glass of water. After taking a seat on a gray sofa, Zak did his best to put the bad dream behind him while contemplating the crew's next move.

Walking home after a visit to a nearby corner tavern, Mookie scanned the dimly lit alley while wrapping his right hand around the .38 caliber revolver in his front coat pocket. Having reached the rear of the property, he opened a rusted, rickety gate, entered the dark gangway, and made his way to the side door. After inserting a gold key into a deadbolt lock, he heard a familiar voice. "Mookie, man. It's Finny." Dressed in all black, Infiniti Ivey emerged from the darkness. "Can I come in? It's important, dog."

The two men entered the hallway and, after Mookie secured the exterior door, quietly entered the lower flat. "Mookie, man" Ivey quietly said, "I need your help. Trey and his boys be after me."

Although Mookie had a good idea why, he acted surprised. "Why? What the fuck's up?"

"The house got hit," Ivey explained. "Trey's puttin' it all on me. Been told he's got an SOS (shoot on sight) out on me. Can you spot me a few hundred? I gotta get my ass out of town, man."

Mookie put his right arm on Ivey's left shoulder. "Yeah, I can spot you $500, but it's all I got at the crib. Wait here." A minute later, Mookie emerged from the living room and handed Ivey $500 in twenty dollar bills.

"Thanks, Mookie, man. I promise to get it back to you. I gotta go. If any dudes come around, tell them you didn't see me and know nothin' about me. Promise me, Mookie."

"I promise, bro," Mookie replied, as he escorted the visibility shaking street tough out of the flat. After securing the exterior side door, Mookie, for the first time, thought about the impact of what he had done. Although they had known each other since grade school, Infiniti and he were not particularly close. Still, Finny had, on occasion, spotted him crack cocaine on credit when money got tight. Now, with the feds in possession of Trey Downing's stash, Infiniti was a marked man. I wonder where he'll go, Mookie thought. Maybe his grandma's in Mississippi.

A half-block south, Ivey stopped in the dimly lit alleyway to dial a cell phone. After ten rings, the call went to voice mail. "This is Gavin Fitzgerald. Please leave your name and number after the tone, and I'll return your call as soon as possible." Ivey placed the device into his coat pocket and continued south through the alley.

CHAPTER NINE

With the crew seated around the kitchen table, Ethan critiqued the group's first endeavor. "The execution was good. We were fortunate they didn't have a camera at the door. If they had, the knucklehead who came to the door may have spotted us lined up along the exterior wall."

"We were also lucky the guy stepped outside," Zak added. "Otherwise, he could have slammed the door shut and we'd have to abort or risk a high-profile gunfight. Overall, though, the execution was very good."

"Using the human shield," Dwyer added, "influenced the response of the second man, just long enough for him to get juiced. That part of the plan was well thought out, and it went down like clockwork."

"Does anyone think they suspected Zak was a bogus delivery driver?" asked Raul.

"I really don't think so," Xavier replied. "My guess is those dudes believe Zak was just happy to get out of there his life. Yeah, nice acting job, Zak. You almost had me fooled."

"Thanks, Xavier. With the debriefing out of the way, what do we have next?"

"I've some info," said Raul. "It's about a garage in the suburbs."

"What suburb?" Ethan asked.

"Brookfield. A guy who leasing a garage with an office attached is packing money into big ass cans of refried beans. The coke comes in from Mexico in refried bean cans. Then, money goes back to Mexico in the supposedly damaged cans of beans, which are resealed in the garage and shipped by truck."

"Has you source actually seen this operation?" Ethan asked.

"My guy's uncle leases the garage where the truck is packed with the resealed cans of beans. The cargo is then taken to El Nino's Supermercado's warehouse near Sixteenth and Bruce. Once it's there, the load is placed inside another truck with actual damaged cans, and it's off to Mexico."

"How will we know when the shipment from the garage is packed and ready for delivery?" asked Zak.

"The truck leaves El Nino's warehouse around 0800," Raul explained, "and is driven to an attached business-type garage near 126th and Lisbon. My source needed a lift to his uncle's garage the other night, and bragged about the thing the entire ride there. Needless to say, he's not the sharpest knife in the kitchen."

"How much money are were talkin'?" Dwyer asked.

Raul smiled. "Five hundred large."

"Holy shit!" Zak shouted. "El Nino's is rolling."

Raul laughed. "You gotta do more than sell tortillas and beans to go from one store to six in just eight years."

"Dwyer," Zak asked, "can you and Raul get some photos of this garage?"

"Sure, we can do that. I have the equipment in my trunk."

"If we do surveillance of the garage on Sunday evenings," Raul explained, "we'll have an idea when the money will move. My guy said there'll be a few cars parked outside the building when the workers pack and seal the cans. Kind of obvious for a Sunday night."

Ethan stood up from the kitchen table. "Okay, there's a lot we need to know. How many people will be at the garage? How many people will be inside the Sprinter? I'm assuming some of them will be well armed. Gently squeeze your source for more info, Raul. We'll have to actually watch them make a delivery to see how it goes down. After what, we can plan and train for the op."

―――――

"Mr. Levinstein," a well-dressed twenty something receptionist said into a telephone receiver, "Your 4 p.m. appointment is here." After setting the receiver down, the woman glanced over the reception counter towards the waiting client. "Mr. Romansky, he'll be right out." The crusty biker, dressed in a black leather jacket and blue jeans, stroked his untrimmed salt-and-pepper beard. Musty was clearly agitated.

Two minutes later, Levinstein emerged from a long hallway

and extended his right hand. "Derrick, come with me." Once inside the attorney's nicely decorated office, Levinstein closed the door. "Have a seat." Musty leaned back in a black leather chair. "I took a look at the discovery," the attorney advised, as he passed a stack of paper across the desk, "and made copies for you."

"I'm tellin' you, Mark," said the biker, "and I'm dead serious: I didn't have any dope. That shit was planted by the cops."

The attorney looked his client directly in the eyes. "I've done some cursory background work on Justin Jacobson, the officer who affected the arrest. He's a twenty-seven-year-old guy with just a few years of experience. He really doesn't match the profile of an investigator that would plant evidence. First off, he would have a tough time getting his hands on a pound of cocaine. Unlike the detectives who do vice investigations, this officer patrols a blue collar area on the graveyard shift. He likely has little contact with individuals dealing large quantities of drugs."

"If the cop didn't plant it," Musty asked, "who did?"

"You've forgotten about the call to the police. You've adamant that you not only didn't point a gun, but you didn't know a gun was in the truck. The DA's office attached the CD of the call to the police with the reports." Levinstein inserted the disk into a computer and played the forty-five second call.

Musty leaned forward. "Hum, I can't say I recognize the voice. Still, whoever called is lying their ass off."

"If we're going to defeat this case," Levinstein advised, "we'll have to identify the caller and show some sort of nefarious intent on his part, defeat the search, or defeat the witness. Since the case has been charged, we now have subpoena power, which one of my investigators used to obtain the caller's telephone records. From what he's discerned, there was only one call placed by the owner of the phone — the one to the police. The phone appears to be a throwaway."

"So what you're saying is I was set up by the cops?"

"Don't assume," Levinstein warned his client. "This is rhetorical question, which means you don't have to answer: how many enemies do you have? Anyone of them could have made that call, and anyone of them, if you're being straightforward with me, could have planted the evidence and made the call. With the call being made from a throwaway phone, our chances of identifying the person are slim to none."

"So how are we going to beat the rap?" Musty asked.

"We have two strategies left: defeat the search or defeat with witness. Since we'll be unlikely to prove the caller and the officer were collaborating, the search, based on the totality of the circumstances, is going to be difficult to beat. When a caller throws the word gun into the mix, most judges are going to see a cursory search of the interior of your truck as reasonable."

"So," Musty asked, "how do we defeat the witness?"

"That's going to be much more difficult. Unlike your previous case, where, for whatever reason, the primary witness caught a bad case of cold feet, police officers will appear in court and are not easily intimidated. I'll file a motion to suppress to the evidence. In the meantime, look over the police reports. If you see anything that merits my attention, let me know."

"Look over the police reports," a fuming Musty mumbled. "Yeah, I'll be sure to do that."

Although it was a Wednesday, The Fallen was packed. Ethan poured glasses of a Champagne knock-off into a dozen glasses. All three Singlaub brothers, off-duty detectives Alex Reyes and Garrett Marks, the detective's wives, along with Zak, raised their glasses. "To Zak." shouted Nick Singlaub. "Happy birthday. To good health and good business!" In the middle of the pub, Raul was busy replenishing a table of food. "Look at that spread," said Nick, as he slapped Zak on the back. "Bet you're glad you took on my suggestion to open a pub?"

"I am," Zak replied, as he slowly snuck away from the off-duty officers and to visit a table tucked in the corner. There, Dwyer and Xavier each polished off hearty cheese and sausage plates. "What did that spot in Brookfield look like?" Zak asked.

"Nothing special," answered Dwyer. "A single car garage, and an office space. The good news is the location is close to major thoroughfares and doesn't appear to be outfitted with any cameras. The bad news: there's other office buildings and businesses in the vicinity, which means potential witnesses at 0800 on a Monday morning. Two of the buildings have surveillance cameras on the roof."

"So," Zak pondered, "do we hit the truck or the building?"

"Once we see the operation go down," Xavier added, "we'll get a better idea. We'll set up there next Sunday with a video camera."

Zak nodded affirmatively. "Sounds good. Have Scrap pour some beers for you. I'm going to say hello to everyone."

Meandering through the thick crowd, the tavern owner felt a sudden tug on his arm. "Zak," shouted Steve Singlaub, "I want you meet someone. This is Griffin Grisby. He's the president of our union, the Milwaukee Professional Police Officers Unit. Griffin this is Zak, the bar's owner."

"Nice to meet you, Zak," said the tall, lanky man, as he extended his right hand. "The place looks great. At a time when so many others are taking aim at our officers, this is a nice tribute to those who've made the ultimate sacrifice."

"Thank you, sir."

"Our office is a few miles north of here," Grisby advised. "This would be a nice spot to visit after our meetings."

"I'd love to have you," Zak replied. "Besides the beer specials for active officers, I'll throw in a pizza on the house."

"That'd be great, Zak." Grisby turned and tugged a man's arm. "Dennison, this is Zak Klatter, the pub's owner. Dennison is the alderman who represents the district just to the north."

The tall, attorney turned politician extended his hand. "Dennison Revis, nice to meet you. I've heard good things about this place. And, sometimes, it's the things you don't hear that stand out, like zero complaints from the neighbors."

Zak smiled. "Thank you, sir. Anytime you want to stop in and checkout us, please do."

When the alderman turn away, Zak slithered to the bar, where Mandy sipped from a cocktail glass. "Sorry that I haven't spent time with you. There's a lot more people here than I expected."

"It's your birthday, Zak, enjoy yourself. Besides, in a few hours, I'll have you all to myself."

"Sounds promising," Zak added, as he gently kissed Mandy's neck.

———

Standing in a grassy area of McGovern Park just north of Custer Avenue, Gavin Fitzgerald looked down at a dead human body. "Damn it, Infiniti, you should've called!"

Homicide Detective LaRon Meeks glanced, skeptically at his colleague. "You know he can't hear you."

"Yeah, I get it," Fitzgerald mumbled. "I told him Trey was going to come after him. I just wonder how much money the 4-5 Mob got out of that house on Lynx. It had to be a substantial."

"Don't beat yourself up," Meeks reasoned. "Thinking about this crazy shit too much will mess with your head. Look, I went to school with a lot of these knuckleheads. They know the risks, but they're stupid enough to think it'll never happen to them."

"By the look of fear on Infiniti's face," Fitzgerald theorized, "they must've caught him by surprise."

Meeks flipped the pages of a steno pad. "At about ten minutes after ten, a woman across the street was watching the local news when she heard doors to a vehicle open. A second later, she heard voices shouting, then heard two gun shots. She got up, peered out her living room widow, and saw a white cargo van leaving at a high rate of speed west on Custer. From the looks of it, my guess is your guy was taking a short cut through the park, was spotted by the people in the cargo van, and confronted. Ivey likely turned, fled on foot back into the park northbound, and was shot in the back. Lying on the ground, he most likely begged for his life before being shot the forehead. Yeah, that look of terror on his face, that'd be life flashing before your eyes."

"Hum," Fitzgerald mused, "I wonder if Trey thought it was an inside job. If Infiniti wouldn't of gotten butt stroked to the head, an inside job would've made sense. After all, the house wasn't ransacked. Whoever did the robbery knew exactly were their stash was. They were in and out. That could explain why Trey doesn't suspect the 4-5 Mob."

"It's a good theory," said Meeks, "but you're filling in a lot of blanks with assumptions. People get blasted for all kinds of reasons, even for posting stupid shit on social media. You could be right or dude could have simply been in the wrong place at the right time. And, if Trey believed it was an inside job, taking out Ivey doesn't make a lot of sense, does it? With home boy six feet under, how's Trey going to find out where his money is at?"

"Trey could be pulling a 4-5," Fitzgerald opined, a reference to the group kidnapping and torturing rival drug dealers for information. "That's why they were out and about in the cargo van, except Infiniti knew what was coming and took his chances."

"Speaking of the 4-5 Mob," said Meeks, "when's HIDTA going to take those shitbird's down? Scraping their dead victims from the pavement is getting old."

"Believe me," Fitzgerald replied, "we're working on it, but you know the feds — nothing happens fast."

—

Had a psychologist analyzed the personalities of the five men operating from the confines of the apartment above The Fallen, he or she would have identified Dwyer Provost as the cast's Achilles' heel. After his wife of seven years left him for a cocaine dealer, the former Navy Seabee began self-medicating with alcohol. He soon traded booze for a sex addiction. Since the kinky sex Dwyer enjoyed was too bizarre for most consensual relationships, he assumed the risk of dealing with the unsavory characters of the vice underground.

In the past, a lack of finances tempered Dwyer's ability to dabble. Things, however, had recently changed. One person who noticed was twenty-four year-old Elena Radulescu. Two years earlier, the Romanian immigrant won a visa lottery and set off for America in search of a better life. Once she arrived, the shapely, attractive brunette with big green eyes discovered she lacked the necessary skill-sets to earn a good wage in a nation awash with low-skilled immigrant labor. Then, she met Moriz, a Russian man who hosted a party at an Oakland Avenue tavern patronized by Eastern European immigrants. The Russian operated a sophisticated network for men on the lookout for sexual hook ups. His workers — primarily immigrant women involved in the sex trade — typically charged $300 an hour, then surrendered a third of their earnings to the Russian middleman, who operated a motel where the "transactions occurred," and maintained a "safety log" of customers and their telephone numbers.

Elena, however, found a way to scam the system. After a few repeat visits, she would schedule "follow up appointments" with a customer off the books at her own apartment. By doing so, she kept the extra $100 for herself. This method of operation came with some risks, primarily because customers' visits to her residence went undocumented.

Dwyer had initially "visited" his Romanian friend five months earlier, but he lacked the funds needed to schedule a follow up appointment on the spot. Suddenly, the bi-monthly visits became weekly visits. Elena once bragged to a friend that one man alone was covering her monthly $1,100 rent. Like a heroin addict, though, Dwyer quickly became immune to what he called "traditional kinky sex," and encourage Elena to take things to another level. As long as he paid in cash, Elena wasn't overly concerned.

Late on Tuesday afternoon, the buzzer to Elena's Farwell Avenue apartment let off its usual obnoxious sound. She buzzed open the building's exterior door for the ever punctual customer, who promised a "bonus" if she "bumped things up a notch." A minute later, Dwyer appeared at the apartment door and was happy to see his host clad in a pair of black boots, black panties, and a black bra. Elena grasped the handle of a three foot long whip in her left hand, and tossed the tail over her shoulder. After Dwyer closed the door, she ran the fingers of her right hand up Dwyer's left leg and grabbed his crotch. Elena moved her tongue in a circle about her lips, stared at her customer, and whispered, "I've been waiting all day for you to give it to me. Take off your shirt." She removed the whip from her shoulder, ran the handle up Dwyer's right thigh, spun her customer around and struck him in the back.

"Ah, Elena," Dwyer moaned, "it feels so good. Harder, babe, harder." But five strikes later, Dwyer still wasn't satisfied. "Come on, bitch," he forcefully said. "Whip me harder." Elena pulled the whip far to her rear and, with all her might, slammed the tail into Dwyer's back. The ensuing crack of the whip opened a small wound on Dwyer's back. "Aw, that feels so good," Dwyer moaned. "Harder, Elena, harder."

Elena, however, had had enough. She didn't mind getting a little kinky when the need existed; however, the last thing she wanted to see was blood from a customer on her small kitchen floor. "No, I'm done. Come and give it to me now."

"Elena," Dwyer moaned, "I'm paying you for this. I'm the customer."

"That's enough," she whispered. "Just let me go down on you."

A look of rage suddenly appeared on Dwyer's face. "I thought we had a deal!" Dwyer bent down, grabbed the whip from the floor, used the whip to form a ligature around Elena's neck, and squeezed.

"Ahhh," the gasping woman moaned, "what you doing?"

Dwyer pulled the ends of the whip together as hard as his muscular arms could. Elena made a gurgling sound, slumped to the floor, and began to turn blue. As if he were possessed by the devil, Dwyer maintained a tight grip on both ends of the whip. Five minutes later, the only witness to the murder was dead.

Then, the euphoria suddenly passed and panic set in. The fantasies Dwyer had experienced for a better part of a year had caused him to kill for the first time. He retrieved and folded the whip, tucked the object in the waistband of his pants, and covered the ligature with his shirt. Then, Dwyer reached for a dish towel and began wiping any surfaces he may have touched, including the door's handles. He peered into the empty hallway, quietly exited, and used the dish towel to pull the apartment door shut. Before exiting the building, the killer wiped the exterior door's handles and buzzer panel. As he grasped the dingy green towel in his left hand, Dwyer causally walked north to Lafayette Place, crossed west at the green traffic light, and made his way, unnoticed, to an older model Chevy Malibu.

———

With a stack of major offense summaries in her hands, Lieutenant Maureen Donnell took a seat at the head of a long, square table to chair the weekly homicide briefing. "We've got a lot on our plate, so let's get started. Meeks and Cortes have caught a couple of hot cases, so I'll let them go first."

Meeks straightened his red tie and glanced down at his notes. "First one up is Infiniti Ivey, a twenty-eight-year-old black male, found dead at the south entrance to McGovern Park — gunshot wounds to the back and forehead. Fitzgerald from HIDTA heard it come over and stopped at the scene. He believes Ivey was the victim of a drug rip at one of Trey Downing's stash houses on the far northwest side. Word on the street has it that Trey's crew was looking for Ivey, so the rip could've been an inside job. Only thing solid so far is the white cargo van fleeing west on Custer Avenue. The autopsy revealed Ivey was shot with a .45 caliber handgun. Today, we're going re-canvass the area and see if the van was caught on surveillance somewhere.

"We're also going to hunt down Maurice Bruce, alias of Mo Mo. He was with Ivey at Trey's stash house on the day of the purported drug rip. Seems pretty hardcore, though. When a copper at the scene asked Bruce who bound his wrists with flexi cuffs and paper sprayed him, his response was, 'Your mama.'"

"Nick," the lieutenant asked, "anything new on the Farwell Avenue deal?"

"We've had a little luck," said Cortes. "The body was discovered by the rental property's caretaker after a man in an adjacent apartment detected a strong odor coming from the victim's apartment. The caretaker called the department, a squad was sent to the scene, and a copper used the caretaker's key to enter, and found the body. The victim is a twenty-four-year-old white female, Elena Radulescu. She was strangled with some type of ligature. The caretaker said the victim is an immigrant from Romania, has received visits from a number of male guests, most of whom are middle-age white males. Based on the kinky porn-type lingerie, the soiled condoms in the garbage can near her bed, and the foot traffic, we suspect prostitution. The ME (medical examiner) believes the victim was dead for about two days."

"Anything on her phone, computer, or on a calendar concerning appointments?" Donnell asked.

"We found a paper list she concealed between the mattress and box spring of her bed," Cortes replied. "It appears she gave her johns nicknames, like Bug Eyes, Hairy Balls, and No Ass. We did find a small stick 'em note with 'Bruce Willis, 4:30' on the front of the refrigerator."

"Using our superior deductive reasoning abilities," said Meeks, sarcastically, "we've concluded the suspect is not the actor, just a similarly looking white male with a shaved head."

"Unless the victim's description is premised on reruns of Moonlighting," said Donnell. The fifty-four-year-old lieutenant looked around the room and noticed the blank stares. "It was a television show in the 1980s when Bruce Willis had hair. Okay, I get it. I'm dating myself."

"We also checked the area for surveillance video," Cortes continued. "Here, we had some success. A camera from a comic bookstore showed a man walking north on the east side of Farwell Avenue at 4:44 p.m., on Monday, which, based on the ME's probable time of death, was the day of homicide. The video is grainy. The man appears to be a white male, in his mid to late thirties, with a bushy beard, and a ball cap. Of course, this being the suspect's image hinges on the 'Bruce Willis, 4:30' note on the refrigerator. We're going to canvass the apartment building and area businesses tonight to see if the man looks familiar to those in the area."

CHAPTER TEN

At 3:07 p.m., the bumper music to Jack Plankinton's AM1020 talk-radio program promptly began. As the music faded, the host introduced the show. "It's mid-afternoon Milwaukee. To some, it's just another day. For those of you tuned in, however, it is a great day because you're *Walkin' the Plank*!"

"Before we delve into the deep state stuff," Plankinton began, "just an observation. Believe it or not, I've been doing this program for thirty years. As time has passed, the newspaper in town has gotten thinner and thinner. We all know the Internet's impact on the print industry, but sometimes, it seems, the newspaper is its own worst enemy.

"Albeit, it took the newspaper three days to get around to covering this story, but it's the reporting that makes me wonder why I continue to subscribe. A young man gets murdered in a public park on Milwaukee's north side. Granted, at the time the crime occurred, kids were probably no longer in the park, but, still, it's a public place. Here's the newspaper's account:

A twenty-four year-old man was found dead in McGovern Park Sunday night. A witness   heard two shots and saw a vehicle leaving the scene. Milwaukee police say the man died from a gunshot wound.

"This is what now passes for a major metropolitan newspaper's coverage of murder in Milwaukee. My first job out of college was a crime reporter in chilly Duluth, Minnesota. When a major crime occurred in the community, I actually responded to the scene, spoke with residents of the area, talked things over with the victim's relatives, and developed sources within the police department. If I would have handed copy of a major crime to the editor containing three sentences, I would've been looking for another job.

"Because of the newspaper's ever shrinking status — last local news reporter over there turn off the lights — many of you have no idea why the rash of recent murders is occurring. Well, I do. If you talk to any Milwaukee cop, they all know why. There's a war going on between gang factions on the north side. What is unusual this time around is the police believe these drug gangs are robbing each other.

"These robberies are much different that say a store clerk or a pizza driver getting held up at gunpoint. The first thing they would do is call the police. For obvious reasons, drug dealers refuse to report the robberies. The only way these incidents appear on the radar screens of investigators is when the police are, for whatever reasons, summoned to the scene, typically by third parties who hear something unusual or stumble upon a body.

"This crime wave is an interesting story that, one would think, the newspaper would want to get out in front of. Instead, the newspaper will simply let the police do the leg work and wait for criminal complaints to be filed. In the interim, the public never hears about the crimes that go unsolved. And how can citizens of a city make educated decisions at the ballot box if they're left in the dark on the issue of crime? Unlike the newspaper, I'll do my best to enlighten my listeners because you're Walkin' the Plank!"

Steve Singlaub greeted a colleague as he entered The Fallen. "Jesus, Joseph, Mary. Look what the cat dragged it."

Gavin Fitzgerald smiled, slapped Singlaub on the back, and took a seat at the bar next to Alex Reyes. "Figured I'd stop for one of the way home. What's the word?"

"Good beer," Garrett Marks replied. "Hey, I heard Jack Plankinton talking about your cases on his show today."

"Plankinton is wired in," said Fitzgerald. "He's shackin' up with Maureen Donnell. If you ever want to get some info to Plankinton, all you gotta do is whisper in the lieutenant's ear."

"What can I get you?" Zak asked Fitzgerald. "I'll have a tapper of Pumpkin Lager." In short order, Zak returned, set a pint on the bar, and stood close by to eavesdrop.

"Do you think the McGovern Park homicide is linked to that drug rip on the northwest side?" Reyes asked.

Fitzgerald nodded affirmatively. "Yeah, Infiniti Ivey. Even though he was a dope dealer, he was personable enough and didn't pull any punches. I interviewed him at the hospital after the rip. I tried to flip him, but he never called. Kind of sad. He's just a statistic now."

"Who's working the case?" Marks asked.

"LeRon Meeks."

"Well, then," Singlaub said, "it's in good hands. Meeks is very thorough. Who's his partner now?"

Fitzgerald thought for a second. "Some newer guy...Nick, what's his last name?"

"Cortes," Reyes answered. "He's sharp kid. He went to high school with my oldest son. The kid was a hell of a shortstop."

"From what I've been told," Fitzgerald added, "all they have to go on is a white cargo van fleeing the scene. I called Meeks after roll call today, but he was on the street following up on that call girl's murder."

"Yeah, that's some strange shit," said Marks. "I read the MOS (major offense summary) — from Romania, strangled to death. No shortage of customers. Eight soiled prophylactics in the garbage can by her bed."

"Probably eight different men's DNA, too," said Fitzgerald, who redirected the conversation. "The more I think about it, I'm beginning to think the drug rip on Lynx was an inside job. The place wasn't ransacked, and why would Trey whack one of his own guys?"

Reyes threw up his arms. "Who knows? It's possible Trey was pissed because Ivey let the money walk. Any idea how much was taken?"

"Not a clue," Fitzgerald replied. "The one witness was an elderly lady who's basically blind without her glasses. All we've got is men dressed in black entering a black van. Infiniti is ten-seven, and his sidekick isn't talking. Still, if the 4-5 Mob was involved, Trey probably would've retaliated by now."

At midnight Sunday, Zak shuttered the doors to the tavern. After Ethan poured each man a tap beer, the weekly meeting began. "Raul, can you give us an update?"

"My guy stopped over last week. After feeding him a few cervezas, he sung like a bird. He once brought an order of food to the garage and was inside briefly while they were packaging the money. It's a three man operation. One man counts the money. A second guy places the money in the industrialized-size cans of refried beans, then seals the cans with a machine. A third man is a lookout. He said there aren't any surveillance cameras in or on the building. The lookout has a pistol. All three are Mexican, but speak decent enough English."

"I've checked the county's Web site," said Ethan. "The property is owned by Yaanay Bushsbaum. He's a Hasidic Jew. I remember him stopping by my dad's yard looking for donations for some cause."

"What's a Hasidic Jew?" Xavier asked.

"Hasidic Jews are Orthodox, which is why I'm surprised Yaanay owns the property. Hasidic Jews participate in the economy to earn a living, but they're supposed to step as far back as they can from the broader culture."

"What kind of Jewish dude are you? Xavier asked.

"My family is Reformed."

"Reformed?" Xavier asked. "So your folks did time?"

Ethan laughed. "It's a religious thing that has nothing to do with the penal system. The point is, since Bushsbaum is the owner, he likely drops by the property to check on his investment, which gave me an idea. If one or two of us dressed in Hasidic garb, the people inside the garage would naturally assume we're affiliated with Bushsbaum, and let us inside."

"That may work for Raul and the rest of y'all," Xavier noted, "but I've never seen a brother the looks anything like an Orthodox Jew. Maybe a Muslim, but an Orthodox Jew, I don't think so."

"I thought about that," Ethan explained. "You'd have to be at the wheel of the van as a lookout."

Xavier nodded in agreement. "Thanks for keepin' it real, Scrap. You know the suburbs. If someone sees a black man standing around outside a business, they'll be five cops there in three minutes."

"We've sat on the place for three consecutive Sundays," Ethan added. "They've gotta be moving that money soon. Once we get an idea of how their operation goes down, we can draw up our plan."

"As far as op on Lynx," said Zak, "I've been eavesdropping on detectives' conversations at the bar. The police have no clue how much money was taken or who was involved."

"And I've noticed the bump in my paycheck, too," said a smiling Raul.

Zak looked down at a sheet of paper. "I should have the rest of the sixty large for Scrap and yourself washed through the business in six months."

"Dwyer, you've been kind of quiet," said Ethan. "You've got anything to add."

"Sorry, Scrap. My ass is kind of dragging."

"Yeah, I see that. You look like shit. Go home and get some rest."

———

At precisely 4:30 p.m., Xavier punched his time card, reached for a thermos, and headed for the door. Three minutes later, his cell phone rang. "Yeah, what up?"

"Have you heard the news, cuz?" Mookie shouted. "One of the dudes from house the feds hit caught a bullet."

"NSA, man, NSA," and irritated Xavier replied.

"What you talkin' about, bro?"

"Never say anything over the phone," Xavier whispered. "Where you at?"

"The gyro place on Oakland and Locust."

"Mookie, man, look for my ride. I'll be there in five."

As he drove west on Locust Street, Xavier was surprised his cousin still believed the feds had retrieved the money from the stash house. He turned left onto Oakland Avenue, spotted Mookie outside, and stopped in a crosswalk. With his passenger inside, Xavier pulled away from the curb. "What up?"

"Finney, one of the dudes who was at the house, caught a bullet in McGovern Park. Word on street has it Trey is pissed off about losing that scratch. Man, now I'm wondering how long it be before one of Trey's boys fingers my ass."

"How much of that thirty-one large you got left?" Xavier asked.

"About twenty-seven."

"Maybe, Mookie, it's time for a vacation. I'll drive you back to your crib. Pack up your money and grab some clothes. We'll put you on a train to Auntie Bell's in Atlanta."

"What about your case, man?" Mookie asked. "If I leave, how you goin' to work it off?"

"I'll stall their asses until you get back," Xavier replied. "For now, they're happy as hell they got that money. Besides the dead dude, who else knows you've been at the stash house?"

"Some punk ass named Mo Mo, but I ain't tight with him."

"Does Mo Mo know where you be stayin' at?" Xavier asked.

"Naw, he ain't never been at my crib."

"Still, it'll be a matter of time before they shout at you. If they find that money up in there, they'll know you were in on it. That'd be a death sentence. Let's grab your shit and get your ass on that train."

Mookie shook his head in disbelief. "What about all my shit at the crib?"

"What's your rent, cuz?"

"Six hundred, but it's not due for three more weeks."

"Give me the money, Mookie. I'll take it over to the landlord on the first."

CHAPTER ELEVEN

Justin Jacobson exited the front door of his Ramona Drive home in suburban Greendale, manually unlocked the door to an older model Chevrolet pick-up truck, and tossed a jacket onto the passenger's seat. The off-duty Milwaukee police officer climbed into the driver's seat, inserted a key into the ignition to fire up the engine, but nothing happened. Damn it, Jacobson thought, the battery must be dead. He then stepped back into the cool morning air and opened the hood.

Across the street, thirty-five-year-old electrician Jay Larson backed out of his garage and spotted a neighbor looking under the hood of a truck. Larson rolled down the driver's side window of his vehicle and shouted, "Need a jump?"

"Sure could," Jacobson replied.

Larson pulled into the neighbor's driveway, opened the hood of his silver SUV, and retrieved a set of jumper cables. He then attached the red and black clamps to the respective battery terminals, returned to his vehicle, and gently put his foot on the gas pedal. A minute later, Jacobson attempted start the truck, but not a sound could be heard. The electrician reached for a flashlight, returned to his neighbor's pick-up, and examined the engine compartment. After spotting something odd, Larson took a knee and glanced under the front bumper. "Oh my God!" the electrician shouted, as he stood upright and moved away from the truck.

"What's wrong?" Jacobson asked.

"I think there's a bomb under your truck."

———

From inside of the captain's office at Milwaukee HIDTA, Detective Garrett Marks stared at the television. "An update on a breaking news story from Greendale," said News 50 anchor Catherine Covington. "Several hours ago, the Milwaukee County Sheriff's bomb squad responded to a residence on Ramona Drive for a report of a suspicious object. After evacuating the nearby area, officers were in the process of examining the device with a small robot when the object exploded. News 50's Abigail Quick is on the scene. Abigail, what can you tell us?"

"Catherine, there's understandably a lot of commotion in this typically sleepy section of suburban Greendale this morning. Police officers say an off-duty Milwaukee police officer could not start his personal vehicle this morning. When a neighbor attempted to locate the problem, he spotted a suspicious object under the truck. An hour later, after the bomb squad arrived and dispatched a small robot, things went south and the object exploded.

"Behind me is what remains of the vehicle." The camera zoomed in on the heavily damaged pick-up truck. "Over to my left, the windows of several homes near the blast site are shattered. Thankfully, though, no one was injured by the blast."

"This is obviously a significant event," a sheriff's department lieutenant told the reporter. "As we continue to process the scene, detectives are checking out all leads."

The reporter looked into the camera. "Catherine, we'll be on scene and offer any updates as soon as they come in."

"Thank you, Abigail. Once again, News 50 is on the scene of a bomb blast in Greendale. No causalities have been reported. So far, officials have not identified a motive or any possible suspects."

"The officer," Marks explained to Captain Steve Jordahl, "is the copper who nabbed Derrick Romansky. Nero's Ignitors is likely up to their eyebrows in this."

"Round up whoever you can and contact the CP (command post)," said Jordahl. "We need to nip this thing in the ass. Targeting rival bikers is one thing, but trying to take out a copper, well, there's going to be hell to pay. This is the United States, not Mexico. Leave no stone unturned."

It took detectives a few weeks to hunt down Infiniti Ivey's former partner, Maurice "Mo Mo" Bruce, who had been laying suspiciously low. Although LeRon Meeks and Nick Cortes weren't naïve enough to believe the street thug would cooperate, the detectives hoped Bruce would open his mouth just long enough to incriminate himself with a pack of lies. Inside a six foot by four foot interrogation room, the so-called "potential witness" had been told he was not under arrest and was free to leave. With Bruce isolated from friends and out of his comfort zone, Meeks began the inquiry.

"Mo Mo, we know you were at the stash house with Infiniti when it got ganked. It's obvious that, besides, Infiniti, you'd be the one with the most to lose. There's not a person on the street who believes Trey would let his money walk without someone paying a price."

"Man, I don't know what y'all be talkin' about," Bruce replied. "Y'all don't know shit. I ain't seen nothin' or heard nothin'."

"Really," Cortes interjected, "because you've been walking around with a very noticeable limp lately. So what happened to your foot? Let me guess, a love tap from one of Trey's goons, right?"

Meeks reached into a manila folder and removed a photograph. "See this, Mo Mo. This is what was left of your guy, Infiniti." Meeks pointed to a large spot in the picture. "Look, his brains sprayed right on out and onto the grass." The hardened gang member noticeably cringed. "And guess who is next? Trey's got one more loose end to deal with. If you don't get your shit together, in a week or two, I'll be showin' pictures of your brains to one of your homies."

"Man, it ain't like that," said Bruce, as tears formed in his eyes. "Finney and me, we was all good with it. I told him not to let any mother fuckers up inside that house."

"Like who?" Meeks asked. "Who ganked your asses?"

"Man, don't be puttin' words in my mouth. I don't know shit about no robbery."

"Don't give me that stupid line of bullshit," said Meeks, sensing weakness. "You were helping Trey hunt Infiniti's ass down, weren't you?"

Bruce suddenly sat upright. "Why you sayin' that?"

Nick Cortes laid a sheet of paper on the desk. "Mo Mo, this is a copy of Infiniti's cell phone records. This number here is yours, right? You called Infiniti twenty-seven times in two days. By the way, you were the last person to speak with him — fifteen minutes before he got blasted."

"You set his ass up, didn't you?" Meeks aggressively asked.

Bruce cupped his face with his hands. "Y'all just make shit up…"

"I don't think so," Cortes replied. "You know, we can ask cell phone companies to track people's locations. So we know you were over at Trey's clubhouse on Hopkins. And we can do the same thing for every phone call you made."

"Now," Meeks continued, "what are we going to find when we get Trey's phone records and compare his locations to yours? The good money says we'll see the two of you in the same spot a couple of times."

"Naw, man," Bruce cried, "this bullshit. Finney was my boy. Y'all really think I want to see him be shot up like that?"

Meeks moved in for the figurative kill. "You got your boy Infiniti to meet you and it was a set up. It was either your ass or his, and you gave him up. Look, I've talked to dozen of knuckleheads like you, and they all think this shit is never going to happen to them. Well, let me tell you something, you're next. Cooperate now and we can still do something for you."

"You know what," Bruce whined, "I wanna leave, man. I want to talk to my lawyer."

"Have it your way," Meeks shouted, "but, during your last dying gasp, remember — I warned you."

The detectives watched Bruce retrieve his jacket, and then escorted him to the door.

Meeks then turned to his partner. "Damn it. I was close. I could feel it. I thought we had him."

———

Like clockwork, at twenty minutes after midnight on Thursdays, Steve Singlaub, Alex Reyes, and Garrett Marks entered The Fallen and bellied up to the bar. With Ethan on his way home, Zak manned the rails. "Now there's a thirsty trio of hardworking detectives if I ever saw them. What can I get you guys?"

"How about a pitcher of Antler Light and three glasses?" Singlaub asked. "Can you throw a cheese and sausage pizza in the oven for us, too?"

"Sure thing," Zak shouted. "By the looks of things on the news, something tells me the three of you have been busy."

"The shits getting crazy out there," Marks added.

"What was the deal with bomb squad in Greendale yesterday?" asked the bartender.

"It's just speculation," said Marks, "but it's likely related to the arrest of Musty, you know, that biker who cut you off. The pickup truck, the one that had the bomb underneath, is owned by an off-duty copper — the guy who arrested Musty."

Zak shook his head in disbelief. "Wow, that's pretty hardcore. Why go after the cop?"

"If they took out the copper," said Reyes, "the bikers would have eliminated the primary testifier in Musty's case. Plus, Musty waived his preliminary hearing, so the arresting officer has yet to offer any testimony that could be admissible at trial."

"Doing something that crazy would have to attract a ton of attention," the bartender theorized.

"Oh, it has," said Singlaub. "The FBI, the ATF, all of law enforcement in the southeastern portion of the state is on the N.I.'s like flies on a cow pie. Everything those turds have done for the past four or five years is going to get a fresh look."

"Still, I'm surprised Musty's people would have went after the copper," said Marks. "Why not try to defeat the case by attacking the search."

"Out of curiosity," Zak asked, "how would they do that?"

"His attorney would file a motion to suppress because the search was premised on the information from the call," Marks replied. "We've looked high and low for any info on the caller, but the number lists to a throwaway phone. I've listened to the call a dozen times. The caller has a slight accent, and is probably Hispanic, but that's about all we have."

"Unless Musty can show the call was a ruse," Singlaub added, "the DA's office believes the search is going to hold up, which is probably why the N.I.s went after the copper. Thankfully, the device was wired poorly and didn't detonate when the ignition switch was turned. The detectives are going house to house and business to business looking for surveillance footage."

Ding, ding, ding, ding, ding. "What was that?" Marks asked.

"Your pizza is ready," Zak replied. "During the week, this is a one man shop after nine." Zak grabbed a hot pad, gently removed the pizza from the oven, and sliced the pie. Turning towards the bar, he saw Mandy enter from the side door.

"Here you go gentlemen," said the bartender, as he set the pizza in front of the three off-duty detectives. "If you need anything else, please let me know." Zak then walked to the far end of bar to greet Mandy.

"What would you like?" Zak asked his girlfriend.

"A glass of orange juice would be fine."

Steve Singlaub turned towards his two colleagues. "Lookout, she's dressed to kill."

"If that red sweater got any tighter," Marks remarked, "she have to iron it on."

After fetching a glass of orange juice, Zak placed his elbows on the bar, leaned forward, and smiled. "I'm glad you made it."

"It's hard to make time for you, Zak," Mandy replied. "You work every night seven days a week."

"I have some good news for you on that front. Scrap agreed to close on Tuesdays, so I can leave around six."

"I would've preferred a Friday or Saturday night," Mandy sighed, "but I'll take what I can get."

⸻

Hyper-paranoid, Dwyer Provost felt a slight sense of relief. A few weeks had passed since the discovery of Elena Radulescu's body, and nothing new had appeared in the local media. Since he resided in the southwestern Milwaukee County suburb of West Allis, the killer was confident east side witnesses, if any existed, would be unable to identify him. On a quiet autumn Sunday afternoon, Dwyer focused a video camera on the Brookfield garage. Seated to his left, Xavier looked on with binoculars.

At five minutes to three, an older model pickup truck parked in a lot on the south side of the building. Ten minutes later, two men in a rented moving truck stopped near the building's garage entrance. When the overhead door came open, the moving truck backed in to the garage, and the door closed. "Finally, some activity," Xavier said to his colleague. "Spending Sundays sitting here was getting old, man."

"Raul's source said it's a three man operation," Dwyer replied, as he snapped photos of the vehicles with a high-resolution digital camera. "So far so good."

Three hours later, a stocky Hispanic man emerged from the garage, walked to the older model pickup truck, and drove off. He returned thirty minutes later and carried a brown shopping bag of restaurant food through the front office door. As darkness set in, the reconnaissance team could see bright lights around the periphery of the office window's closed blinds. Dwyer reached for a yellow walky-talky and an ear piece, then handed another radio to Xavier. "I'm going over there to check it out. If we can see lights, I should be able to get a glimpse of what's inside. If you see anything, give me a shout."

Dressed in a black ball cap, a black pullover sweatshirt, and blue jeans, Dwyer walked across the lightly traveled street and entered the parking lot. After removing a flashlight from a rear pants pocket, he examined the interior of the older model truck in the parking lot. After extinguishing the light, Dwyer maneuvered his stocky frame along the south wall of the building, stopped at the office window, and looked through a crack in a bamboo woven shade. The door from the office to the garage portion of the building was half-open.

Suddenly, the ear piece cracked to life. "Popo coming up on your six." Dwyer followed the south wall, ducked down, and concealed himself behind the front tire of the truck opposite the approaching officer. The black and white Brookfield police cruiser slowly drove by, continue north, made a U-turn, passed by the building, and left the area. Xavier depressed a button on the walky-talky. "It's clear."

Dwyer returned to the office window. Looking through an

opening in the blind, he observed a Mexican man in cowboy hat with stacks of money in each hand. Seconds later, the man with the money disappeared from view. Having confirmed there was cash inside, Dwyer returned to the van, opened a side door, and stepped inside. "Oh, yeah, they've got stacks in there. As far as Raul's info is concerned: two for two so far. By the looks of it, they're going to pull an all-nighter."

"Cool," Xavier replied. "I'll shoot Zak a call so he can relieve us at 2300 hours."

———

As Zak caught twenty winks, Ethan kept tabs on the Brookfield garage. At 6:45 a.m., the building's overhead garage door opened, and the rented moving truck, with one occupant, moved out of the garage. After checking to make sure he had captured the vehicle on video, Ethan nudged Zak with his foot. "Hey, we had some movement. The moving van just took off. There should be just two guys in there now."

"Alright," a groggy Zak moaned, "I'll take over. I'll wake you up if and when the delivery vehicle shows up."

Ethan gave up his seat, slid over to an adjacent chair, and wrapped a blanket from his feet to his neck. "Sounds like a plan."

An hour later, an El Nino's delivery truck came to a stop in front of the garage and beeped its horn. "Scrap, it's here." As Zak operated the video camera, Ethan zoomed in on the delivery truck and the driver, and then snapped dozens of photos. Within a minute, the delivery truck had backed into the garage and the overhead door closed.

"How long do you think it will take to load up five hundred large stuffed in cans of refried beans?" Zak asked.

Ethan threw up his hands. "How the hell would I know? But I'll bet there's at least two guys in the back of that delivery truck armed to the teeth."

Thirty-seven minutes later, the overhead garage door opened, and the El Nino's truck left to make its apparent monthly deposit.

CHAPTER TWELVE

As his partner, La'trell "Boo Boo" Triplett, stood lookout, Marcus "Mobie" Webster locked the exterior door of the 4-5 Mob's Locust Street after-hours tavern. "Those crazy mother fuckers dropped some serious bank on those nasty-ass holes we got at the club."

"Yeah, they sure did," said Triplett, as he surveyed the area for potential threats. "If they've wasn't so fucked up, anyone of those dudes could've got those holes for a ten dollar rock (of crack cocaine)."

Then, the side door of a nearby van slide open, and a hail of gunfire erupted. Struck once in the stomach, Triplett feel to the pavement, rolled onto his side, retrieved a .45 Smith and Wesson semi-automatic pistol from his waistband, and returned fire. Armed with a short barreled shotgun he had concealed under a three-quarters length jacket, Webster took a knee and fired three one ounce slugs at the attackers. In a matter of seconds, the van fled east towards 27th Street.

Inside the Milwaukee Police Department's communications center, a ShotSpotter alarm alerted a District Seven dispatcher. "Fourteen thirty-four, ShotSpotter alert. Multiple gunshots two-nine and Locust."

"Fourteen thirty-four," Officer Jason Brock replied, "ten-four. At two-seven and Locust. Got a van moving at a high rate of speed northbound on two-seven. Be advised, the van just lost control turning right at Burleigh, left the road, and slammed into a gas pump."

"Fourteen fifteen, out at the scene with fourteen thirty-four. The van just burst into flames. One in custody. Two others inside the van. Need fire A.S.A.P."

———

"So what's inside this bag of shit?" Lieutenant Maureen Donnell asked a group of uniform officers and detectives gathered around a bank of tables inside the Investigations Bureau. Called in to assist, Detective Gavin Fitzgerald went first. "Based on what we found at the scene — the lot adjacent to the 4-5 Mob's after-hours — it appears Webster and Triplett just closed the place down and were ambushed by Trey Downing's crew. We found Triplett's blood just outside the building's door, along with five expended forty-five caliber casings and two expended twelve gauge shells. In the street, where the van was parked, we found five nine millimeter casings and eight forty caliber casings."

"I talked to my partner at the hospital," said Nick Cortes, "and the statement he got from Triplett more or less confirms what was found at the scene."

"What do we have with the van?" Donnell asked.

"The guy in custody is Maurice Bruce," Brock replied, "alias of Mo Mo. He's the lucky one. The other two, LaJohnson Gregory, alias of Juju, and Tecumseh Jones, they're crispy critters."

"My partner and I, recently interviewed Mo Mo concerning the Infiniti Ivey homicide at McGovern Park," added Cortes. "When LeRon gets back from the hospital, we'll take another crack at him. This time around, we'll have some leverage."

"Gavin," the lieutenant asked, "you've been working the 4-5 Mob. What's going on here?"

"Back in summer, the 4-5 Mob allegedly robbed one of Trey's runners near sixtieth and Appleton. A squad responding to an unrelated report of shots fired in the area spotted the car used in the robbery moving at a high rate of speed near fifty-first and Center. They gave pursuit, and caught one of the 4-5s in Calvary Cemetery. One of the coppers spotted a duffel bag being tossed from the fleeing sedan near fifty-fifth and Garfield. An informant said a hundred grand was in the duffel bag."

"A great find for someone," Donnell quipped.

"A white male was captured on the squad's dash cam when the duffel bag was tossed," Fitzgerald explained. "He's probably the lucky recipient. There was another probable drug rip on Lynx, too, where Trey lost a yet to be determined about of cash. While the jury is still out on who's responsible for that one, tonight's shooting, at a minimum, is retaliation for the Appleton robbery."

—

"Mo Mo, my man," LeRon Meeks shouted. "We've got you jammed up good this time — recklessly endangering safety, felon in possession of a firearm, attempt first degree intentional homicide — I could add more." Like a condemned man being led to the gallows, Maurice Bruce looked down at the floor. "Before we get started, I'm putting our cards on the table. We've got two members of the 4-5 Mob who've put a gun in your hand, but here's where you really messed up: you didn't see the surveillance camera on the outside of the building. It captured everything. Now, my partner read you your rights, but before we can kick this around, we need to know if you're willing to answer questions without legal counsel present."

"What good's it gonna do me anyway," Bruce replied. "Ain't no lawyer gonna un-fuck this."

"So, knowing your rights as my partner read them, are you willing to answer questions?"

"Yeah, I'll answer questions, but only if y'all do something for me."

"Like what?" Cortes asked.

"Okay, if I tell you what you want," said a shaking Bruce, "I'll be a dead man."

"Here's the thing," said Meeks, "I can't promise you anything I can't deliver. However, something tells me I'll be very interested in what you've got. Once I have the details, I can run it up the flag pole. That's all I can tell you for now, my man. If you got a good card, now's the time to play it."

"The stuff I know about Trey," said Bruce. "You know, the drugs and money. Them cappin' Finney, and, yeah, the shit that went down today."

"Alright," Meeks replied, "here's what I'll do. First, we'll talk about today's incident. Then, if it's okay with you, I'll have some other detectives join us. Once they're here, we can kick around the big picture stuff. You good with that?"

Bruce's right hand began to shake. "Yeah, man, whatever."

"So why were the three of you blastin' it out of that van on Locust Street today?" Meeks asked.

"Trey was pissed cuz those 4-5 punk asses robbed some of our spots."

"Where did these robberies occur?"

"One was over on Sixtieth," Bruce replied. "They was wearing masks and jacked Juju when he was gettin' in his ride."

Meeks leaned forward. "What'd they jack him of?"

"A green duffel bag with a hundred big ones and a key."

"How did Trey know it was the 4-5 Mob?" Cortes asked. "There are lots of idiots out there doing drug rips."

"Trey knows a lady cop," Bruce replied. "She told him some 4-5 dudes got rid of the bag when y'all was chasing them in a car."

"A lady cop?" Meeks asked. "What's her name?"

"Shaniqua, but I don't know her last name. She be a sergeant."

Meeks looked at Cortes, wrote the sergeant's name on a sheet of paper, and passed it to his partner. "How does Trey know Shaniqua?"

"Ah, man," Bruce sighed, "she's been blowing up Trey's phone for a while, even took him to Jamaica."

"So, what happened today was Trey getting back at the 4-5's for the drug rips, right? Meeks asked.

"Yeah, them 4-5 dudes be pissin' lots of people off. Trey thought they did the house up on Lynx, too, the one I was at, but I dunno."

"What do you mean, you don't know?" Meeks asked. "You were there. You don't think it was the 4-5 Mob?"

"Man, check this out, this is how it went down. A driver from Chicken Wings Unlimited came up to the door with a delivery, except we didn't order shit. When I opened up, they hit me in the face with pepper spray. Thing is, the wing's driver was a white dude. No way he could've been standing at that door without seeing those mother fuckers along that wall."

"A white dude?" Meeks asked. "Are you sure."

"As sure as I'm here now," Bruce replied. "A pasty ass white dude. The motherfucker who shouted at us inside, he was a brother, but the dude at the door was white."

"So the delivery driver was there when the robbery when down?" Cortes asked.

Bruce sat back in his chair. "If you're asking me, I think the driver was in on it, man. He begged for his life and shit, but then, when the dudes who jacked us left, he took off. If he was a straight up delivery driver, why didn't he call the police?"

"How much money did Trey lose?" Meeks asked.

"Over three-hundred big ones. We put it up in a hole in the wall behind the stove, but you're boys never looked up in there."

"Did you tell Trey about the white delivery driver?" Cortes asked.

"Sure did, but Trey thought the white dude was legit; that he probably got scared and shit, and was just glad he got out of there without getting his ass shot. Trey thought it was the 4-5s. He checked with Shaniqua. She told him y'all didn't know who it was."

"If Trey thought the house got ganked," Meeks asked, "why did he have his boys blast Infiniti?"

"Man, Trey is one paranoid, dude. I was walkin' back from the store when four of his crew kidnapped my ass and stuffed me inside a van. They took me to the clubhouse over on Hopkins, taped me to a chair, busted my foot, and shit. Trey wanted to know if we had let any dudes that wasn't supposed to be there up in the house. I told him Finney had let a few in. Trey thought one of the dudes Finney let in was a snitch for the 4-5s. Man, I'm tellin' you, they knew exactly where that money was at."

"So those phone records I showed you the last time we talked," asked Cortes, "did you make those calls to Infiniti to lure him to the park?"

"Trey gave me two days to find Finney or he was going to cap my ass. So, yeah, I made those calls, but I wasn't there. Whatever happened to Finney is on them. Then, Trey told me that, since we lost the money to the 4-5s, me and Juju — one of the dudes in the van when it crashed — needed to make good for losing his money by shooting up the 4-5s spot on Locust today."

Meeks scribbled a note and passed it to Cortes. Tell the lieut to get a hold of Fitzgerald to help debrief Mo Mo. Let her know what we've been told about Shaniqua Barkley, and explain the info will not appear in any of our reports. Cortes read the note and left the interrogation room.

Inside the dingy warehouse, Ethan showed the crew a mock-up of the Brookfield garage. "Based on the Intel, Zak and I have kicked it around and think its best do hit the place on Saturday evening. The most opportune time is if and when one of the guys leaves to make a food run. If that happens, we'll have about a twenty-five minute window. If we're still inside when he returns with the food, we can take him by surprise when he walks in."

"What if he doesn't leave for food?" Dwyer asked.

"We'll wait until 1900 hours," Zak explained. "If he doesn't leave for food by then, we'll go with the same plan and just have to deal with three men instead of two."

"What's the plan to get inside?" Raul asked.

"Zak and I will be dressed in Hasidic garb," Ethan explained. "Dwyer will look like an electrician — work shirt, ball cap tool belt, etc. We'll paint his beard black and wear some thick black glasses for disguise. I'll have one of those magnetic placard signs made up to slap on the van to make it look legit."

"Great," Dwyer replied, "I guess I'll be shaving my beard before I go to work on Monday."

Ethan laughed. "It'll grow back."

"When Ethan and I go to the door," Zak added, "we'll tell them we're there to check on an electrical problem. If they're smart, they'll ask why they weren't given a twenty-four hour notice. If they do, I'll hand them a bogus notice, allegedly drafted the day prior, and claim we slid it under the door and, for whatever reason, they didn't see it."

Ethan walked to the building's office door mockup. "This is where it gets dicey. If we get inside, Dwyer will pepper spray the person or people who came to the door. But if one guy is still in the garage and hears his partner in the office screaming, he'll be coming right at us packing heat. That's why one of us has to have a set of eyes of the garage entry into the office prior to those inside the office getting hit with pepper."

"What if the dude at the door doesn't open up or won't let you in?" Xavier asked. "What then?"

"Ethan will make the call," said Zak. "At that point, he'll decide if we should force our way in or abort. If we abort, we probably won't get another kick at cat. You can bet whoever leases the building is going to call Yaanay when we leave."

"Where will I be?" Raul asked.

"If they see your face," said Zak, "they'll correctly suspect that, since you're Mexican, you're the one that provided the info for the robbery, which my tip off your source that you're involved. So you'll be armed and masked in the back of the van. Once we have the place secured, we'll open the overhead garage door. If they have a vehicle parked inside, Dwyer will move it out and Xavier will back the van in. Dwyer will provide cover while Ethan, Raul, and I load the van up."

CHAPTER THIRTEEN

"According to Bruce," Gavin Fitzgerald explained to fellow detectives Alex Reyes and Steve Singlaub, "Trey's crew tracked down two of the three men Infiniti let inside the stash house — street names of Lil Dre and Peabody. After giving them the once over, Trey doesn't believe they're involved, which leaves only one man left — Mookie. Our database has forty-one black males listed with the alias of Mookie. Based on the description and age range Bruce provided, I've trimmed the number to thirteen. I'm going to show Bruce their booking photos this afternoon."

"Any idea why Trey's people haven't gotten to Mookie?" Singlaub asked.

"Bruce has been kept in the dark on that, so we're unsure why. But if we can find Mookie, and he talks, we'll know who did the robbery."

A perplexed look appeared on Reyes' face. "I thought you said it was the 4-5 Mob."

"Based on the info Bruce provided, things have changed. On the night of the robbery, a white, male delivery driver was on the stoop with an order of wings no one at the house had ordered. Bruce was then hit in the face with a blast of pepper spray by someone just feet away from the delivery driver."

An inquisitive Singlaub leaned forward. "So the delivery driver and home invaders are co-conspirators?"

"I'm not sure," Fitzgerald replied. "According to Bruce, Trey doesn't think the white male is involved."

"Is it possible the 4-5 Mob enlisted the help of a white guy?" Reyes asked. "That sure would've thrown Bruce and Ivey off."

"I don't know," Fitzgerald answered, "but my gut tells me this Mookie character can fill in a lot of blanks."

———

Nick Cortes tossed a white envelope from the Wisconsin Regional Crime lab onto his partner's desk. "Finally, some news on the Radulescu homicide," Cortes told LeRon Meeks. "We got a white, male DNA profile developed from the two small spots of blood on the kitchen floor of the apartment."

"Any hits from the state or CODIS (the FBI's combined DNA index system)?"

Cortes shook his head. "Nothing, but the DNA recovered from the used rubbers in the trash can doesn't match the blood on the floor."

"So he killed her before they had sex," Meeks thought aloud.

"Maybe the rough foreplay wasn't enough for him," Cortes theorized. "Fantasy sex is driven by the fulfillment of the fantasy, whatever it is. Could be that murder, not a sex act, was the actual fantasy."

"Anything on the grainy photo?" asked Meeks.

"So far, there's nothing from the canvass of the building or from people who live in the area. The lieutenant is leaning towards releasing the photo to the news media with the hopes of generating new leads, but I've been pushing back. The whip Elena used on her customers is missing. It's the likely ligature used to strangulate her. The way I see it, the killer took the whip with him. These pervs love trophies. If we can somehow ID him, it would be nice to get a search warrant and find that whip inside his place."

"It sure would," Meeks added. "And if the perpetrator sees the photo on TV and thinks we're getting close, he'll destroy the evidence."

Cortes nodded in agreement. "My thought, exactly."

———

As the sun set, Xavier used a key to open the exterior door's deadbolt lock to Mookie's flat. He quietly shut the door, scaled five, creaky steps, and fiddled with a set of keys. A woman peered through the crack of her second-floor unit and caught a glimpse of a man entering the first-floor apartment.

Using the light from a cell phone, Xavier walked through the kitchen, entered the living room and found the area ransacked. I knew it, Xavier thought. It was only a matter of time before Trey's boys figured out where he lived. Xavier felt his heart begin to race. Shit, Xavier thought, Trey's people are watching this place. He quickly exited the rear door, checked the dark gangway, and made his way out of the building. Once in the alley, Xavier climbed inside his Dodge Durango and drove north. At the end of the alley, he turned right and soon was traveling west on Vliet Street.

Seconds later, a white cargo van came to a stop two doors south of Mookie's flat. Two men, both with pistols concealed under their jackets, made their way to the same door Xavier had exited a few minutes earlier. The woman from the upper flat opened the exterior door, and invited the men into the hallway. "He up and left a few minutes ago," said the woman.

"Was it Mookie?" one of the men asked.

"It's dark up in here, and the landlord don't fix the lights," the woman replied. "So I couldn't tell y'all for sure."

One of the men removed a wad of cash from his pants pocket, peeled off two, one-hundred dollar bills, and handed them to the woman. "You did us right. Call again if you see anything."

The woman smiled as she placed the bills in her bra. "I'll do that."

Having unknowingly got away unscathed, Xavier turned onto Hawley Road en route to The Fallen. Though he had hoped Mookie's troubles would soon pass, it was time to tell Zak that Trey Downing had fingered their informant.

When Xavier arrived, he took a seat at the unoccupied end of the bar, and was spotted by Ethan. "What's up, Xavier?"

"I gotta talk to Zak."

A scowl formed on Ethan's face. "You know we're not supposed to talk shop here."

"I know, Scrap, but it's important."

"Hang on," said the bartender. "I'm going get you a beer and a menu. Do your best to come off as a customer."

A minute later, Ethan returned with a glass of beer and set a menu on the bar. "What gives?"

"I was just at my cousin's place. His crib's been tossed. At first, I didn't say anything to you, but I got this feeling Trey's boys were onto him Mookie. So I put him on a train to our auntie's house in Atlanta."

"So, at least for now," Ethan asked, "he's out of harm's way, right?"

"Yeah, I think so. Doubt they could track him down there. So where's Zak at?"

"He's on a date with Mandy," Ethan advised, "and I don't want to ruin his night off by calling him. I'll leave a note and ask him to give you a jingle at 1000 tomorrow. Now, put some money on the bar," Ethan instructed. "I'll make change for it at the register and bring it back." Xavier slapped a ten dollar bill on the bar, which Ethan carried to the register. A few seconds later, the bartender placed a five dollar bill and five singles in front of Xavier. "When you finish the beer, skedaddle. You can bounce it off of Zak tomorrow."

"I'll do that, Scrap. Thanks for the beer, man."

———

Zak entered Mavis' Coffee Shop, where he spotted Xavier seated at a corner table. After ordering and receiving a cup of cappuccino, Zak took a seat at the table. "Sorry to bother you, Zak."

"It's not a problem. Scrap is covering for me at the pub. What's up?"

"Trey's boys are looking for my cousin."

"What makes you think that?" Zak asked.

"One of the dudes at the house we hit caught a bullet in McGovern Park," Xavier explained. "I was thinkin' Trey must've thought the dudes at the house got played by someone who had been there. So I put my cuz on a train to Atlanta. Last night, I checked on his crib, and it had been tossed. I had a feeling it wouldn't take long before Trey would find out where he was at and come lookin' for him."

"So, what you're saying, Xavier, is that your cousin is tucked away."

"As far as I know, yeah. I called our auntie's house last night to warn him. He's gonna stay with her for awhile."

"Okay," Zak mused, "so for now, at least, it's all good. Is he talking to anyone up here and telling them his whereabouts?"

"He's freakin' out, so I don't think so."

"Keep tabs on him," Zak advised. "When you speak with him, explain that it's best if he keeps his pie hole shut. Another thing: do not go back to your cousin's house. If they ransacked the place, someone is probably lying in wait for him."

"What about all the shit he's got up in there?" Xavier asked.

"What does he have there that's of any value?"

Xavier thought for a few seconds. "A big screen, computer, and a bedroom set."

"Are those things worth dying for?" Zak said sarcastically. "Consider it a loss. After all, we just gave him thirty-one large."

"Yeah," Xavier sighed, "you're right about that."

"It'd probably be a good idea to touch base with him every now and then," Zak advised, "but we need to move forward and stay focused on the next op."

Lieutenant Maureen Donnell entered room 325 at the City of Milwaukee's Safety Academy, which houses the police department's Internal Affairs Division. A well-groomed sergeant, dressed in a white, dress shirt and blue necktie, glanced up from his desk. "What can I help you with, lieutenant?"

"I'm here to see the captain."

"Send her in," shouted Captain Moses Grinnell, a tall, former, Division I college football offensive tackle. Donnell walked into the captain's office and closed the door. "So you've heard something about Shaniqua Barkley?"

"Her name came up during a QP (questioning a prisoner) by two of my detectives," Donnell confirmed. "According to the informant, the sergeant is romantically linked to a big-time drug dealer, Trey Downing. The informant went on to say Barkley passed along details about a duffel bag — believed to contain one hundred grand and a kilo of cocaine — tossed from a fleeing vehicle during a police pursuit last summer. The duffel bag was allegedly taken during a drug rip from one of Downing's dope houses. According to the source, the sergeant told Trey a rival gang, the 4-5 Mob, did the job. The coppers apprehended a 4-5 member involved in the pursuit."

"Between you, me, and these four walls," said Grinnell, "we've heard certain things about Sergeant Barkley, but we haven't been able to corroborate the allegations."

Donnell slid a manila folder across the captain's desk. "The informant said Barkley has called Downing a number of times, and even went to Jamaica with him."

"Guilt by association alone won't cut it," said the captain, in a deep, steady voice that reverberated off the walls. "To make something stick, we'd need incriminating statements on tape. So far, the information we've received has come from sources with credibility issues. However, if you're willing to play ball, we may be able to develop what's required for a wire."

"What do mean by play ball?" Donnell asked.

"The Tiburon system," Grinnell explained, "allows those with the rank of captain or above to restrict which members of the department can see certain reports. These constraints usually apply to homicides, sensitive crimes, and anything at HIDTA or narcotics. My guess is Barkley got access to the reports involving the duffel bag because the incident was written up as fleeing an officer. As you know, a personal log-in is not currently required for non-restricted reports unless they're printed. However, a personal log-in is required for the AIM system, which allows any supervisor to track use of force complaints and things like squad accidents. I don't want to get into specifics, but, when the need exists, one of my investigators — with the authorization of the chief, of course — would create a use of force report authored by you, with your consent. An IT administrator would then restrict access to the report in the AIM system to Sergeant Barkley only."

"Now I'm following you," said the lieutenant. "When she passes the details along to Downing, you can prove the info came from only one person."

"Exactly. In the past, while conducting surveillance of Barkley's departmental computer activity, our people learned that she has sought to use the AIM system as a backdoor to defeat Tiburon's restrictive access. In most instances, supervisors filing use of force reports have adhered to policy. As a result, the information inputted into the AIM system has been limited to use of force issues only. Still, to prove misconduct in public office, we need to show Barkley is acting as a conduit for Downing."

"Alright," Donnell agreed, "If it means getting a dirty cop off the street, I'm willing to play ball then."

CHAPTER FOURTEEN

"Gentlemen," Zak bemoaned, as he leaned back on a kitchen chair, "what we have here is a staffing problem. It's football season, and I can't close the pub on short notice at five in the afternoon on a Sunday. There are customers at the bar until nine or ten."

"So what you're saving," Raul interjected, "if we hit the garage on a Sunday evening, it'll be a four-man job."

Zak nodded affirmatively. "And the only two people who can manage the bar are Scrap and I."

"In that case," Ethan offered, "I can work the bar."

"I don't think that'd be a good idea," Zak replied. "You're off on Sundays. If I simply disappear on a Sunday evening, the regulars might find it unusual, including some of the law enforcement types. If word of the op gets out, they may somehow put two and two together. But if I'm at the bar, they won't suspect a thing."

"If we roll four deep," Ethan said, "we'll need to revisit Raul's role. Since his source provided the Intel, I wanted to keep his profile as low as possible."

"We could add a guy," Dwyer suggested. "I know someone I could approach."

"Absolutely not," Ethan objected. "We need to limit the number of people involved. We can do this with four people. We'll just need to work fast. We can't expose Raul's face, though, which means he'll have to stay in the van and mask up. Dwyer and I can dress in Hasidic garb. We'll use Xavier as the electrician."

"You sure about that, Scrap?" Xavier asked.

"Believe me, you'll look like a genuine tradesman in that uniform, tool belt, and ball cap," said Ethan. "We'll disguise you with a fake mustache and black rimmed glasses."

"What about logistics?" Zak asked. "You need a minimum of fifteen minutes to get the van from the garage in Brookfield to your uncle's warehouse, which, by the way, is only a mile east of one of El Nino's locations."

"It's one of the X factors," Ethan acknowledged, "but based on what we've observed, once the food runner returns, there are no other visitors. Let's meet at the warehouse at 0600 on Monday morning to prep for the op."

———

Inside a small hotel room in the suburb of Oak Creek, Gavin Fitzgerald laid twenty manila folders on a desk. "Since you couldn't ID Mookie from the first set of photo arrays," the detective explained, "I put together some more. Take your time."

After Maurice Bruce passed through the first ten photos, Fitzgerald began to think the effort was a colossal waste of time. Then, upon opening the second to last folder, the man in witness protection stared at the photo. "This is him."

"Are you sure?" Fitzgerald asked.

"Damn straight. He looks a little younger, but it be Mookie."

"How sure are you," asked the detective asked, "like fifty percent, sixty percent, or what?"

"Man, I ain't playin'. One hundred and ten percent it's Mookie."

Fitzgerald compared the number on the booking photo to a list of names in his notebook. "Dinkins Danbury," Fitzgerald marked. "With a first name like Dinkins, I'd use the alias of Mookie too."

"Yeah," Garrett Marks chuckled, "the nickname of Dinky wouldn't go over well with the ladies."

Fitzgerald reached for a cell phone and called the Investigations Division. "Hello, Amber, this is Gavin Fitzgerald. Please do a work up on Dinkins T. Danbury, black, male. Date of birth of seven, seventeenth of ninety."

———

Zak looked at the clock, which read 12:20 a.m. Steve Sinlaub and his friends should be arriving any minute now, he thought. Less than five minutes later, Singlaub stepped through the door followed by Alex Reyes, Garrett Marks, and Gavin Fitzgerald. The four men removed their jackets and placed them over the backs of stools at the bar. "What's it going to be tonight?" Zak asked.

"Start us out with a pitcher of Antler Light," Singlaub said, "and, if you could, please toss a couple of pizzas in the oven. We're expecting a couple more people."

"Sure thing. A pitcher and two pizzas coming right up." As he filled the pitcher of beer, Zak, standing four feet from the detectives, eavesdropped on their conversation.

"Meeks and Cortes wanted to compare notes," Fitzgerald told the other detectives, "so I invited them here for an unofficial debrief. Those two have done some excellent work worthy of beer and some pizza." As Zak placed four glasses and the pitcher of beer on the bar, two men entered through the front door and approached their colleagues.

"Welcome to The Fallen," Singlaub shouted. "Pull up a chair."

"This place is nice," said Meeks. "I live over at sixty-sixth and Center and didn't know it existed."

Singlaub stood up. "Let me introduce you to the owner. Zak, this is LeRon Meeks and his partner at homicide, Nick Cortes."

Zak extended his right hand across the bar. "Zak Klatter, nice to meet the both of you. Homicide detectives, wow, from watching the news, you two must be busy."

"You know what they say," said Cortes, "our day begins when your day ends."

Zak laughed. "So true. There's nothing more permanent than a dirt nap. So, what can I get the two of you?"

"A couple of glasses would be fine," said Meeks.

"I've ordered a couple of pizzas, too," said Singlaub.

When the two new arrivals filled their cups, Fitzgerald proposed a toast. "To the detective work of LeRon and Nick."

"Here, here," Marks shouted. Each man bumped their glasses and took a swig of beer.

"I've got some good news for you," said Fitzgerald. "I've identified Mookie — the man Trey's people believe was in on the drug rip on Lynx." Wiping the bar a few feet away, Zak listened intently as Fitzgerald continued. "He's Dinkins Danbury. We made his residence near fortieth and Vliet, but no one answered. A woman in the upper-level said he hasn't been there for a while. According to Bruce, Mookie is the only person unaccounted for as a snitch in the drug rip."

"Well, hopefully we get ahold of Mookie before Trey's people," Cortes said. "It's odd that the white guy was in on it. Did Mo Mo give you a good description of the delivery driver?"

"Sure did," said Fitzgerald. "About six foot, mid-twenties, fit, probably a hundred-eighty-five pounds, clean shaven, wearing thick, black glasses. We offered to bring in a composite artist, but Bruce said it happened so quickly that his recall, prior to his getting hit with pepper spray, was — pun intended — sketchy."

"That's a fairly generic description," said Singlaub, as he looked at the bartender. "Shit, it sounds a lot like Zak."

"What was that?" Zak asked, even though he had heard the conversation.

"Steve said the description of a suspect was so vague it could've matched you."

"Well, you know what they say," Zak quipped, "we white guys all look the same." The five detectives and Zak shared a hearty laugh.

Meanwhile, Zak's mind raced like a mental patient pacing a padded room. This Mookie, he thought, has got to be Xavier's cousin. If they find Mookie, they'll soon learn about his cousin, Xavier, who is allegedly working for the feds.

—

"Let's think this through," Ethan told Zak, as he sipped from a cup of coffee. "This Downing character and the police both know who Mookie is, but neither knows where he is. If either the dope dealer or the police find Mookie, he'll likely identify Xavier. Yet Mookie, who believes Xavier is working for the feds, doesn't know our identities."

"And Downing," Zak added, "believes Mookie is a snitch for the 4-5 Mob."

"Then the only way for us to avoid being identified is to get rid of Mookie."

"Really, Scrap, you want us to off Mookie? What would Xavier think about that?"

"Xavier would probably rat us out, which is why we can't do Mookie. Someone else has to."

Zak shook his head in disbelief. "Like who?"

"It can't be Trey's crew," Ethan theorized. "Before killing Mookie, they'd torture the shit out of him, and they'd find out about Xavier. The outlier is Trey's rivals."

"The 4-5 Mob?" Zak asked.

"Yeah, the 4-5 Mob. We know they rob dope dealers and leave a trail of bodies behind. What we need is a premise to make the 4-5 Mob believe Mookie ripped them off."

"I've heard a couple of the detectives talking at the bar about the 4-5 Mob," said Zak. "Last summer, the group robbed a member of Trey's crew of one hundred large and a kilo of coke. The police chased the robbers' car, and a duffel bag full of cash and the coke was tossed from the car. The police suspect some bystander stumbled upon it."

Ethan's eyes looked upward. "Interesting, very interesting. What if we put a bug in the 4-5's ear that Mookie got hold of the duffel bag and, with the money and the coke, left Milwaukee for Atlanta? What do you think the 4-5 Mob would so?"

"They'd probably hunt his ass down," Zak answered.

"Exactly. We both know Mookie recently came into possession of a decent sum of money. The 4-5 Mob has no incentive to search for anything but the money and the person who, indirectly, ripped them off. Did the detectives say when the duffel bag was tossed from the car?"

"This past summer," Zak answered.

"Well, then, one would expect a majority of money would be gone, but Mookie would still have a chunk of it, right?"

"I suppose so, Scrap, but your plan has two major flaws. Atlanta is a big city, and neither of us knows Mookie's precise location. And we sure as hell don't have any connections inside the

4-5 Mob."

"If we're deceptive enough," Ethan surmised, "we can get Mookie's location from Xavier. As for the 4-5 connection, well…"

"Wait a minute," Zak recalled, "there was in the newspaper about the 4-5 mob a few weeks ago. One of the detectives that stops in with Steve Singlaub mentioned it while bullshitting at the bar."

"Find the article and forward the link to me. I'll see what I can come up with. In the meantime, we need an address for Mookie."

CHAPTER FIFTEEN

"I know you mentioned it before," Dwyer moaned, "but I'm sick and tired of sitting here every Sunday. This shit is really getting old."

Xavier glanced over at the passenger seat. "Patience, my man. I don't like it either, but it'll all be good when we get paid."

"I sure as hell hope so. Raul and Scrap are home watching football. Zak is at the bar, is we're sitting here. When we're finished with this job, I'm going to tell them you and I need to see a little extra in our stacks."

"Dwyer, why you so uptight, man? We've pocketed a chunk of change, and drink for free. So far, this gig's been the cat's meow."

"Well, I got needs."

"Dude, what you need is to finish that newspaper. You've been starin' at the same damn page for an hour." Xavier glanced down at the local section and spotted several columns dedicated to the murder of Elena Radulescu. "What a damn shame."

"What's that?" Dwyer asked.

"That girl getting killed. It's a damn shame. I heard about it on the TV news. Some people on the east side are sayin' it's a serial killer. What do you think?"

"Ah, ah, ah," Dwyer stuttered, "I don't know."

"Come on, man," Xavier laughed. "You've been lookin' at that article since we've rolled up. You gotta have an opinion about it. I'll tell you what I think: whoever murdered that girl is one sick puppy. I bet he killed her cuz he couldn't get a stiffy. What's your take?"

"How the hell would I know? What do I look like, Doctor Phil?"

"To kill some time at Camp Lejeune," Xavier explained, "I read a book by one of the agents who started the FBI's psychological profiling unit. So here's my profile of the killer: A white guy, pushing forty, who has problems holding a job. Quiet, but not a loner. Those close to him would say he's a little distant. Always seems a bit on edge. Dude's got a serious problem with women."

"Can you shut the hell up and focus on the damn garage?"

"Sorry," Xavier mumbled, "all I was tryin' to do was make the time pass."

———

Xavier and Dwyer walked through the side door at The Fallen, took seats at a corner table, and patiently waited for the last customer to leave. Zak locked the doors behind the exited customer, went to the bar, and took a pitcher of beer and three glasses to the table. "How did it go?"

"Boring as hell, to say the least," Dwyer replied.

"Yeah," Xavier added, "dead quiet over there."

Dwyer chugged his beer, slammed the glass on the table, and stood up. "Thanks for the beer. I'm going to take off. My ass is draggin'."

"What's up with him?" Zak asked.

"He's pissed off we're spending our Sundays sitting on the garage."

"It does suck," Zak offered, "but sitting in a warm SUV for six hours is hardly bustin' rocks."

"Man, I gotta take a squirt. I'll be right back." When Xavier made his way to the men's room, he left his unlocked cell phone on the table. Zak reached for the device, checked the recent calls section, snapped a photo of the list, and set Xavier's phone in its original spot. A minute later, Xavier returned and took a seat.

"Have you heard anything from your cousin?" Zak asked.

"I've called him a few times. Seems like all is well and good."

"Cool. By the way," Zak carefully inquired, "you never told me your cousin's name."

"I don't know why, but we've been callin' him Mookie since I can remember. To tell you the truth, after he had to leave, I felt kind of bad about puttin' him in a tough spot. But now that he's in Atlanta, I think gettin' him away from Milwaukee was a good thing."

"Well," Zak reasoned, "hopefully it's a win, win then."

Xavier raised his glass. "Yeah, to Mookie!"

"To Mookie!" Zak toasted.

Nick Cortes knocked on the front door of a two-story flat in the 1800 block of North Marshall Street. "Who is it?" asked a woman, in broken English.

"We're detectives with the Milwaukee Police Department," Cortes explained. An attractive blond woman in her early twenties cracked open the door. "I'm Detective Cortes and this is my partner, Detective Meeks. We'd like to speak with Janina Adomaitis."

"What you want to know?" the woman asked.

"My partner and I are investigating the murder of Elena Radulescu."

"I Janina," the woman said, as she pulled open the door.

"Could we step inside to speak with you?" Cortes asked.

"Come in, yes."

When the detectives crossed the threshold, Meeks noticed that, prior to closing the exterior door, the woman placed her head outside to check for possible onlookers. "We've spoken with several people about Ms. Radulescu," Cortes said, "and your name was mentioned as someone who'd kept in close contact with her."

"Elena, she my friend, yes."

"We know that you work, like Elena did, for the Russians. My partner and I work homicide, not vice. As far as our investigation is concerned, we're interested in what you knew about Elena, not what you do for a living. Do you understand?"

"I understand, yes," Janina replied, as she looked towards the floor in shame. "I tell you what I know."

Cortes opened a steno pad. "What's your birthday?"

"I born March 18, 1995."

"From our conversations with others," said Cortes, "we've been told that you emigrated from Lithuania."

"I come here in 2016, summertime, yes."

"How is it that you knew Elena?"

"Me and Elena, we go to Shorewood tavern. I see her some-times. We meet Russian man, Moriz. He tell us we can make mon-ey working for him, so we do. Elena live not far from me. We become friends, share stories. We miss our families, our friends."

"Did Elena ever talk with you about her customers?"

"She do. Sometimes we laugh. Sometimes she scared, wor-ried. I tell her not to have them at apartment, but she not always listen."

"So you looked out for her," said the detective, seeking to soothe the witness's concerns. "That's something friends would do for each other. We've noticed that she gave her customers nick-names. Did she ever mention this to you?"

"She make me laugh by that, yes. One guy she call, ah, needle dick. Things we do at times not make us happy, no, so have to laugh sometimes."

"We do the same thing," the detective responded. "When my partner and I see a mangled body, we'll make a wise crack. We're not being disrespectful, just trying to minimize the cruelty that gets under our skin. Did she ever mention a man that she had nicknamed Bruce Willis?"

"She do, yes. Man, ah, how you say, shaved hair. Said he visit a lot. Pay lots of money. Enough to pay rent."

"Okay," said Cortes, as he jotted down notes. "Did she say anything else about this Bruce Willis character?"

"He like whip, yes, not sex much. Elena think he not funny guy. How you say, I think, serious. No joking. Would pay $50, too, for Elena to give panties, put over his head, smell them."

"So he was really odd?" Cortes asked.

"Not so much than others," Janina explained. "Lot of men want, how you say, kinky. Why they visit, not go home to wife."

"Did Elena ever describe this man to you?"

"What you mean, scribe?"

"Did she say what the man nicknamed Bruce Willis looked

like?"

"He look like Bruce Willis. That why she call him that."

Meeks busted his partner's chops. "Hello, Captain Obvious."

"Okay, I understand that," said Cortes, "but anything like height, weight, the way he talked, anything?"

"Don't think so, no."

"Do you know how she scheduled visits with her customers?" Cortes asked. "Did she use her cell phone?"

"Think she first met at Moriz hotel, then invite to apartment. Once guy come over first time at apartment, then make another time when he come back. Phone she got from Moriz, wouldn't use for apartment guys. Moriz find out, Elena in trouble."

"Does Moriz have a list of Elena's customers?"

"Think so, yes, but Moriz not give, I think."

"Well," Cortes grinned, "we'll see about that."

Suddenly, the woman's eyes teared up. "You find who kill Elena, yes? Bad way to die. I miss her much. She my friend. Her family, do they know?"

"Not yet. The Romanian consulate in Chicago is still working on that. Here's a card with my name and telephone number. If anything else comes to mind or you hear something, please give me a call."

After being shown to the door, Cortes turned to his partner. "What a damn shame — these women get sucked into this bull-shit."

Meeks nodded in agreement. "Sex is big business. Maybe Elena's murder will serve as a   wakeup call for Janina."

Working The Fallen's bar alone on a Tuesday, Ethan watched as two dozen customers entered the front door. The bartender recognized only the man who approached. "Hello, detective. What's going on tonight?"

"We just came from our monthly union meeting," Gavin Fitzgerald explained.

"Cool. I'll get you set up and throw a couple of pizzas in the oven for you gratis."

"You don't have to do that," Fitzgerald said.

"No, really, let me get the pizzas for you, detective. I'm at the bar by myself on Tuesdays. With the neighborhood not being the greatest, I'm glad you and your co-workers decided to stop."

"Well, thank you, ah…."

"The name's Ethan, sir."

"Please don't call me sir," Fitzgerald joked, "I work for a living. Gavin will do. When you get a chance, can you bring over three pitchers of Antler Light and three pitchers of Bull Moose Amber?"

"Will do," Ethan replied. "From what I've been reading in the newspaper, you guys must be staying plenty busy, huh?"

"What article are your referring to?"

"The one about that gang," Ethan specified, "where one of the leaders hunted down witnesses and threatened to kill them."

"Oh, yeah, the 4-5 Mob. I'm actually one of the detectives working them. They're some tough nuts to crack."

"Why is that?" the bartender asked.

"First and foremost, as the article mentioned, people are fearful of them. They also have one of the most unethical attorneys in the state on retainer. When something goes down with the 4-5s, like magic, Neil Dermod is there within a half hour."

"Dermod," Ethan thought aloud, then asked, "is he Jewish?"

"I'm pretty sure he's not," the detective replied.

"Good, at least they can't blame my tribe then."

"If it makes you feel better," Fitzgerald laughed, "I think he's a member of my tribe — the Irish."

———

The following day, Ethan arrived at The Fallen a half-hour early and spotted Zak restocking the bar. "Hey man, when you have a chance, we need to talk."

"Okay, hang on a minute." Zak poked his head through the kitchen's service window. "Raul, could you watch the bar for a few minutes. I have to grab a few things from the basement."

"Yeah, sure thing," the head cook said. "Scrap, you're in a little early."

"I wanted to grab something to eat before work," said Ethan. "Could you fire up a cheese burger for me?"

"One world-renowned cheese burger coming right up."

Ethan then followed Zak down a flight of steps into the basement to report his findings. "I went online and found an address that lists to the 404 area code number you photographed on Xavier's phone. It belongs to Bessie Danbury on Lois Place NW in Atlanta. Xavier's placed nine calls to this number in five days. This has got to be the address where Mookie is staying."

"You're probably right. Xavier told me he's called his cousin a number of times recently. So how do we get the info to the 4-5 gang?"

"Last night," Ethan explained, "Gavin, the Milwaukee detective, stopped in with some other people after a union meeting. When he came to the bar, I asked him about the article in the newspaper. He's knows the 4-5 gang well, and said they have one of the most crooked attorneys in Wisconsin on retainer — a guy named Neil Dermod. I checked him out online. He has a law office on Wisconsin Avenue. So I got to thinking: why not send a hand written note to the Dermod saying a guy named Mookie, who has since fled town, has in his possession a green duffel bag that his clients are looking for at a certain address in Atlanta? If Dermod is as crooked as the detective believes, he'll pass the information to the gang."

"Damn, Scrap, you're one devious bastard. Hope I never end up on your shit list. After your shift ends, can you stick around until close?"

"Sure, no problem. I'll have a few beers, and we can take care of this afterwards."

CHAPTER SIXTEEN

Seated around a table inside a HIDTA conference room, Vance Rathman, an agent with the federal Bureau of Alcohol, Tobacco, Firearms and Explosives (BATF), walked investigators through the forensics of the Greendale blast. "The explosive device — C-4 housed inside a six-inch-by-eight-inch metal casting — was attached to the drive shaft of Justin Jacobson's truck. The device was relatively sophisticated, and used with a high-tech mercury switch as the detonation instrument — set to go off when the vehicle moved. It has all the hallmarks of Nero's Ignitors."

"We're working on an affidavit for a wiretap," Garrett Marks told the other members of the biker task force, "but we still need to run it up the chain of command at the DOJ."

"Meanwhile," a police lieutenant added, "we have a two-person security detail watching Jacobson's residence twenty-four, seven. Needless to say, his wife is a little shook up, as are others in the neighborhood."

"Musty is apparently hell-bent on beating his dope case one way or the other," said Marks. "So the feds have taken some extraordinary steps."

"The bar on Stewart Street the N.I.'s visit after meetings is for sale," Rathman explained. "Big Bill Wellesley, the former owner of Snap's Tap in West Allis, was popped with two hundred and forty pounds of weed he brought up from Texas. Fortunately for us, Big Bill's home caught fire. When firefighters extinguished the flames, they stumbled upon a dozen, large, metal containers packed with high-grade marijuana. At age fifty-seven, Big Bill doesn't want to sit in prison until he's eligible for Social Security. He flipped and is working for us. The DOJ has given Bill the funds to purchase the Stewart Street tavern. Of course, he'll shut it down for a few weeks to remodel, at which time we'll have the place wired. If someone at a corner table so much as drops their ass, we'll have it on tape."

Seated at a computer terminal inside the sergeant's office at

District Seven, Shaniqua Barkley used her department ID to log into the Milwaukee Police Department's AIM computer network. Once the program opened, she placed Officer Jason Brock's name into a search menu. The first entry, case number 18-292915, was a police use of force versus Maurice Bruce. Barkley right clicked the mouse to view the report authored by Lieutenant Maureen Donnell. Hmm, the sergeant thought, why would an Investigations Bureau lieutenant file a use of force report for a street officer? After thinking it through, Barkley saw it plausible that a homicide lieutenant would file such a report because the incident was related to a death investigation. Although the document contained details outside the purview of a use of force, the sergeant attributed the additional information to the lieutenant's lack of street-level supervisory experience.

As she scanned through the document, one particular item caught Barkley's attention: the cellular telephone recovered from the now cooperating Maurice Bruce was said to contain "previously deleted incriminating images of Trey Downing." The device was placed on "inventory pending a forensic examination to retrieve said images." Lieutenant Donnell's report noted the inventory number for the cellular telephone, which was stored at a warehouse two miles west of police headquarters. The sergeant took notes from the report, walked outside the district station, and placed a call from her personal cell phone.

"It's a go," an excited Dwyer Provost told Xavier, as the rented moving truck pulled into the garage, and a dark blue sedan parked adjacent to the building.

Xavier reached for his throwaway cell phone, went to the contacts section, and selected the number for Jerry.

"Yeah," Ethan answered.

"It's moving day," Xavier said in a pre-arranged code. "We're ready to go."

"Okay, when we're in position," Ethan explained, "we'll let you know. Sit tight until we get there. I'll get a hold of Kramer."

Ethan left his west side apartment and drove to his uncle's

warehouse. When he arrived, Raul was waiting in a nearby truck. Once inside the large building, Raul swapped out the van's license plates, placed four equipment bags in the rear of the vehicle, and slapped magnetic placards for D & G Electric on both sides of the vehicle. In short order, Ethan emerged from a small office dressed in a circular, black, fury cap, a fake beard, a white dress shirt buttoned to the collar, and a black suit.

"Scrap, man," said an impressed Raul, "you really look the part."

"I hope so. We've got to step on it and get over there. Did you pack Xavier's and Dwyer's disguises?"

"It's all here," Raul confirmed. "I checked everything on the list." With Raul behind the wheel and Ethan seated on a rear bench seat, the van left the warehouse.

Twenty minutes later, Xavier's throw away phone rang. "Meet us at the pre-arranged spot." Xavier drove his red Durango into a parking lot behind a closed car dealership on the north side of Capitol Drive. Once inside the van, Ethan used a toothbrush and black shoe polish to darken Dwyer's dishwater-blond beard as Xavier donned the electrician's uniform, black-rimmed glasses, and tool belt.

"Xavier," Ethan asked, "do you have the revolver and the canister of pepper spray?"

"Sure do. The revolver is in the tool box, and the pepper spray I got hidden under the tool belt."

"And I've got the sawed-off (shotgun) slung around my shoulder under this coat," Dwyer advised.

Xavier looked at Dwyer and laughed. "Dude, that funky brimmed hat, fake curls, and black beard could fool anybody."

"We can critique the disguises, later," Ethan remarked. "Let me see your hands. Okay, we're all gloved up. Let's go over the basics one more time. We'll park in the lot across the street. If their guy doesn't leave to make a food run by 1800 hours, we'll move forward regardless. Once we're inside, Xavier's going to spray the guy who lets us inside with pepper. Dwyer, you'll be covering the door from the garage into the office with the shotgun, and I'll be covering, too, with a pistol. Once we have their people secured in flex cuffs with hoods over their heads, Raul will drive the moving van from the garage and back our van inside. Dwyer will cover the subdued men with the shotgun, and the rest of us will load the money into the van as fast as possible. Any questions?"

"What about my ride?" Xavier asked.

"This parking lot is filled with cars from the dealership's repair shop," Ethan said. "The Durango will blend right in. I'll drive you back early tomorrow morning before anyone from the dealership arrives. We'll swap out the plates, and you'll be on your way."

"Alright," Xavier replied nervously.

Ethan glanced at his colleagues and sensed each man had butterflies in their stomachs. "Let's take a few deep breaths and, at least for the time being, take it down a few notches. We've drilled this op a dozen times. We're well prepared. We have the advantage of surprise. And remember, although time is of the essence, smooth is good. Is everyone ready?" Raul, Xavier, and Dwyer nodded affirmatively. "Okay, now let's kick some drug dealer ass."

Raul drove the van to Lisbon Road, turned east, and backed into a parking stall across the street from the intended target. An hour-and-a-half later, a Hispanic man emerged from a glass office door and made his way to the blue sedan. "Here we go," Ethan told the crew. "Once he leaves, we'll have twenty-five minutes to get in and out before he returns."

With the sedan out of sight, Raul drove across the street, and parked adjacent to a windowless, brick wall. Ethan, Dwyer, and Xavier exited the van's sliding side door and approached the office door. Ethan peered through the glass and, after seeing no one in the office, rang the doorbell. Seconds later, a stocky Hispanic man with tattooed arm sleeves approached the door. "Sorry, we're closed," the man shouted through the glass, not knowing what to make of the two Hasidic Jews and the black man with the tool belt.

"We're not customers," Ethan shouted. "We're here on behalf of the building's owner, Yannay Bushsbaum, to check on some faulty wiring."

"I don't know nothin' about it," the man said. "We got no notice."

Ethan held up an eight-inch by eleven-and-a-half-inch sheet of white paper. "I slid this notice of inspection under the door yesterday."

"Sorry, man, but I'm not lettin' anybody in. We're busy."

"In that case," Ethan threatened, "I'll have to call the police. This is an important matter. If the wiring isn't checked, the building could start on fire." Not wanting the police anywhere near the money packing operation, Ethan could feel the wheels churning inside the man's head.

"Where's the electric problem at?" the man asked.

"Inside the office, along the south wall."

"Okay, I'll let you in," the man relented, "but only in the office. We're busy working in the garage and don't need anyone bothering us."

Ethan tugged down on the ends of the circular shtreimel hat that extended to his false beard. "That's fine, sir. The reason we're doing the inspection on Sunday is Mr. Bushsbaum didn't want to disrupt weekday business."

The man turned the lock, pushed open the glass door, and watched the three men enter. "So where's the problem?"

"It's coming from that wall socket," Xavier mumbled, in an effort to conceal his voice.

The man bent over and glanced towards the wall. When he turned around, Xavier hit him in the face with a blast of pepper spray. "Ahhhhhh, what the fuck!" the man screamed. Five seconds later, a thin, Hispanic man, who had entered the garage with a silver pistol in his hand, was greeted by the sawed-off shotgun Dwyer had pointed at his face.

"Move and you're fuckin' dead!" Dwyer screamed. "Drop it, and get on your belly."

The man complied, and, as Ethan checked to ensure the garage was clear, Xavier placed flex cuffs on the second man's hands before placing a black hood over his face. As Xavier finished securing the man who had opened the door, Ethan shouted, "All clear!" Dwyer and Xavier pulled the two men into the garage, and placed them on the ground with their backs against a wall. With the shotgun in hand, Dwyer covered the prisoners.

Ethan peered inside the moving truck. "Hey, over here," he whispered to Xavier.

"D-a-m-n," Xavier mumbled, "that's one big-ass pallet of cash. How much you think is there?"

Ethan shrugged his shoulders. "I don't know, but, by the looks of it, I'd say at least a million."

Exiting the office door, Ethan stepped outside and gave Raul a thumbs up. The black van moved across the sleepy Sunday street and parked alongside the building. Raul then entered the building and met Ethan inside the office. "Change of plans," Ethan advised. "Most of the money is still in the back of the moving truck. There's so much, we won't have time to swap it out. The keys are inside the truck. Jump inside and drive it to the warehouse. We'll meet you there."

Raul donned a ski mask, entered the garage and climbed inside the driver's seat of the truck. Ethan pushed a button and watched as the overhead door opened. In a matter of seconds, Raul removed his hood and drove off south towards Capitol Drive.

As Dwyer and Xavier watched the two men, Ethan approached and whispered in their ears. "It's a rap. Let's hit it."

"What about the money inside those cans on the counter?" Dwyer whispered.

"Forgot about it," Ethan replied. "Most of the money is inside the moving truck. I'll go outside to make sure it's clear. Then, I'll pull the van over to the office door, so you two can jump in."

On a slow, Sunday evening, thirty-four-year-old Luke Horn patrolled the area north of Lisbon Road in a Brookfield police cruiser. Ahead to his right, Horn spotted a man in a funny looking black cap and black suit step from the office of what appeared to be a closed business. Horn pulled into the parking lot, rolled down his passenger side window, and stopped near a black van marked with D & G Electric placards. "Good evening, sir. Officer Horn with the Brookfield Police Department. It's unusual to see much activity over here on a Sunday night. Is there a problem?"

With his hands in plain sight and a pistol concealed in the rear waistband of his pants, Ethan slowly approached the squad car to speak with the officer through the window. "Nothing we can't handle, officer. The tenant alerted us about an electrical problem, and we're having it checked out. I'm Shneur Bushsbaum. My uncle owns the building, but he's away on business in New York."

"Must be a big problem to have an electrician come out on a Sunday," the inquisitive officer responded.

"We're Orthodox Jews, officer. Our Sabbath begins at nightfall on Friday and ends at nightfall on Saturday. It's not unusual for our religious practices to be misinterpreted."

Not wanting to appear culturally insensitive, Horn dropped his guard. "Sure, no problem. I understand."

"And we wouldn't be here on a Sunday," Ethan explained, "if my uncle didn't feel the problem was important. He was fearful the electrical problem could start a fire."

"Well, then," the officer replied, "I'm glad to see that you're taking care of it."

Ernesto Cuellar turned right from Lisbon Road, and spotted a police cruiser stopped outside the garage. When he brought the sedan to an abrupt stop, a brown bag — containing tacos and refried beans — slid off the front passenger's seat and onto the floor. Cuellar pulled the car to the curb and watched as a man dressed in Hasidic Jewish garb spoke with the police officer. Thirty seconds later, the police cruiser pulled away. The man in the strange black cap then turned and waved to someone inside the building. When the glass door opened, another man, also dressed in Hasidic attire, as well as a black man in a uniform, exited and quickly walked to a nearby black van. Seconds later, the vehicle sped off towards Congress Street.

"Damn, Scrap," said a relieved Dwyer, "that was close. You must have given that cop a good line of shit."

"I'm glad he left, but, when I was talking to him through the window, I noticed he was wearing one of those body cams, and it was pointed right at me."

"Good thing you had on a disguise," Xavier remarked.

"We all know it's unlikely the dope dealers will call the cops," Ethan said, "but, if that camera was on, it captured my voice."

With the black van gone, Cuellar drove to the front of the building, where he found the glass office door unlocked. Once inside, his lungs became slightly agitated and he began to cough. Upon entering the garage, he spotted his colleagues bound with hoods over their heads. Before assisting the two men, Cuellar reached for his cell phone to alert his boss.

Twenty minutes later, as the black van approached the warehouse, Ethan spotted the rented moving truck in the parking lot. Ethan entered the warehouse, opened an overhead garage door, and waved Raul inside. "Dwyer," Ethan asked, "check to see if the rental van has a GPS tracker. We'll start offloading the money."

Dwyer reached for a flashlight and looked under the rental vehicle's dash. After checking each of the truck's wheel wells, he opened the hood and saw nothing was hardwired to the battery. "No GPS system," he yelled.

Ethan let out a sigh of relief. "Thank God. I didn't even think about it until we left the garage. Last thing this warehouse needs is a visit from a Mexican drug cartel. But here's the thing: if they haven't done so already, you can bet El Nino's will have anyone it can muster looking for this truck. Dwyer, once we transfer the money to my uncle's transport truck, take the moving van over to Kaszubes Park on Jones Island. I'll swap out the plates on that seventy-seven Cadillac over there, and Xavier will follow behind you. On the way back, take a victory lap. Pick up some grub for us at the El Nino's deli on Sixth and National. We'll stay put until 2200 hours, then take the transport truck to Zak's garage to count the booty."

———

"Gary," Zak asked the last remaining customer, "you waiting on a ride?"

"Yup, I called for a cab."

Zak patted the man on the shoulder. "Good deal, man. Hey, it looks like the cab just rolled up."

In his mid-forties, Gary stood up and staggered towards the door. "See you on Friday."

With his last customer gone, Zak locked the front and side doors, shut down the kitchen, slipped out the back door, and entered the rear garage. Five minutes later, he heard the transport truck roll up and opened the overhead garage door. Ethan carefully backed the vehicle into the garage, and the overhead door closed. Dwyer opened the rear doors of the transport truck and ripped a brown tarp off the loot. "Holy shit!" Zak shouted. "Talk about the motherlode."

The crew quickly emptied the large carry bags of their equipment and filled the sacks with the cash. Thirty minutes later, each man carried a bag up a flight of steps to Zak's apartment. Ethan placed the bag on the sofa, reached inside, and removed two handfuls of unbound cash. "What we need is a name."

"What are you talking about?" Zak asked.

"They've got Trey's crew and the 4-5 Mob," Ethan explained, "but we've got no name. Every team needs a name."

"Hey, Zak," Xavier shouted, "what's the name of the dude who robbed those banks after he got discharged?"

"Nico Walker?"

"Yeah, Nico Walker. Dude had PTSD and robbed ten banks. Man, I bet homeboy would be proud we ganked these dope dealers."

"He probably would," Ethan reasoned, "but what does that do for us?"

"Like our veteran brother, Nico, as misguided as he was, we're warriors!" Xavier shouted. "Yeah, that's who we is — we're Nico's Warriors."

Ethan laughed, threw handfuls of money into the air, and, as the cash fluttered to the floor, shouted, "Nico's Warriors it is!"

After dividing the money into stacks, the crew spent the next three hours passing the various numbers to Zak, who tallied the sum. With the final numbers displayed on a calculator, Zak looked around the kitchen. "Does everyone have a beer?" When the four others raised a bottle, Zak presented the total. "Okay, you're not going to believe this, one point five million and a few thousand in change." Zak held up the calculator, which read 1,510,250. A toast: to Nico's Warriors!" The five men bumped the bottles together. "Now, there's the question of how to divide the booty. Since I wasn't there to assume the risk, I'll leave it to the four of you."

"I move to give Zak ten percent," Ethan motioned. "He's the mind behind the operation."

"I agree," said Raul. "Since Xavier and Dwyer did most of the leg work on this one, they should split the other ten percent Zak would've gotten."

Ethan concurred. "I'm good with that."

"That's more than generous," said a smiling Dwyer.

"I'm cool with it, too," Xavier added.

Zak reached for the calculator and divided the numbers. "Okay, after the twenty-five dollars you guys, ironically, dropped for dinner at El Nino's: Xavier and Dwyer each get $377,550, Scrap and Raul each $302,050 each, and my take is $151,025. Not a bad haul. And this time, we've got no snitch to pay."

"Look," Ethan told the crew, "we're dead tired, and I know it's not the time for a personal finance lecture, but a decent sum of money like this shouldn't be left lying around."

"I have plans for mine," Dwyer noted. "I talked a guy into selling his small vending machine company to me. All I need is thirty grand down, and I'll wash what I need through the company."

Ethan nodded affirmatively. "Excellent plan. After all, Zak can only launder so much through The Fallen."

"Yeah," Zak added, "if I ever get audited, it's going to be tough to justify paying a full-time bartender a hundred grand a year, without tips. The head cook, well, I can exaggerate Raul's hours and claim to have paid out a ton in overtime."

CHAPTER SEVENTEEN

Mookie slammed the interior door of his aunt's Lois Place Atlanta home and strolled down an unkept path to the street. On an unusually cool morning, he took some comfort seeing the sun break through a patch of clouds. At Jones Avenue, he turned left towards a neighborhood outreach center that sponsored a daily food giveaway. As he passed Ruth Street, the man in hiding saw nothing unusual about a maroon conversion van parked near a wooded hill littered with garbage. Had he paid closer attention, the vehicle's front Wisconsin license plate would have sent up a red flag.

As Mookie continued down on the sidewalk-less, residential street, the maroon van turned onto Jones Avenue and swerved in front of its intended target. When the van's passenger-side door slid open, the pedestrian was greeted by two masked men, one of whom was armed with a sawed-off shotgun. After being pulled inside, the butt of the shotgun slammed into the back of Mookie's head and he lost consciousness.

A few minutes later, the 4-5 Mob's Jeremiah "J.B." Barnes, Khalil Jackson, and La'trell "Boo Boo" Triplett stood in front of their naked captive. Inside a small warehouse, Mookie found himself strapped to a wooden chair, his arms and legs bound with thick cellophane wrap. A cheap, plastic football helmet — shoved backwards, over his head — obstructed his vision.

"Ah," Barnes shouted, "you there?"

"What the fuck?" Mookie moaned. "What the fuck's going on?"

"This is how it is," said Barnes, in a stern voice, "all we want is the money. We know you got the money."

"Man, I don't know what the fuck y'all takin' about."

Khalil Jackson lit a Phillies Blunt cigar, took a few puffs to ensure the ember was hot, went to a knee next to Mookie, and shoved the hot cigar into the captive's left testicle. "Ahhhhhhhhhhhhh, f-u-c-k!" Mookie squirmed in the chair, as Barnes and Triplett held him down.

"This can be as painful as you want it," said Barnes. "All we want is the money."

"What money?" Mookie shouted.

Jackson raised Mookie's testicles and shoved the hot cigar into his scrotum. "Ah, shit! Mother fuck!"

"Don't be playin' us like that," Jackson sneered. "We're here for the money. Stick' em in the balls again."

"Hold on, man!" Mookie shouted. "Alright, man, I'll tell you where the money be at, but you gotta promise not to hurt my auntie. She got nothin' to do with it."

"If we get the money," Jackson explained, "it's all good, bro. Once we have it, we'll let your stinky ass go."

"Alright, man, alright. I'll tell you where it's at. The scratch is in a metal box buried on the side of my auntie's house in a flower bed with a statue of Jesus above it."

"All of it!" Jackson screamed.

"All I got left is in there."

"It better be," Jackson warned, "or we'll fuck your auntie up, come back here, and bust your knee caps."

"I'm tellin' y'all the truth. It be right where I told you."

Jackson turned to Triplett. "You stay here and watch him. We'll get the money."

Mookie listened intently, and heard two men exit through a door not far behind him.

"Now, keep your ass quiet and sit still," said Triplett. "Otherwise, I'll bust you in the ribs with a baseball bat."

"I'm cool," Mookie mumbled.

Within a matter of minutes, the warehouse became silent. Then, Mookie heard his captor begin to snore. Mookie shoved his head sharply backwards, which moved the loosely-fit football helmet from his eyes. The man in front of him was resting comfortably on a tattered sofa with a baseball bat to his left and a black pistol to his right.

With his knees bound to the chair, Mookie slowly stood as far as he could, hunched over, and arched the chair over his back.

He carefully turned and spotted a door that appeared to open by depressing an aluminum bar in the center. He then inched his way to the door, turned around to ensure his captor was still asleep, and nudged the chair on his back against the aluminum rail. Mookie felt the door open, and the cool air collided with his unclothed body. He slowly backed into the door until his body wedged through the opening. He then frantically hopped through the rear parking lot of the Brady Avenue warehouse towards busy Marietta Street, with the bouncing plastic football helmet partially obstructing his vision.

Inside the warehouse, La'trell Triplett heard a door slam, opened his eyes, and observed that Mookie and the chair had vanished. Triplett reached for the pistol and exited the rear door. Looking to his left, he observed the escapee, naked and still attached to the chair, just feet from Marietta Street. Triplett raised the gun to eye level and fired four rounds. With bullets whistling past his head, Mookie hopped as fast as he could towards the busy thoroughfare. A red car in the right lane of westbound traffic spotted the naked man and came to a screeching halt; however, an SUV traveling the same direction in the left lane continued forward, slammed into the naked pedestrian, and sent him airborne. Mookie was dead before his body hit the ground.

—

Just before dawn, Mandy pulled back a heavy quilt, rolled out of Zak's bed, and walked through a dark hallway to get a glass of water. At the point where the hallway met the living room, her right foot came in contact with a hardwood floor flush reducer. The groggy woman tripped and fell on the living room floor. In an effort to boost herself from the floor, Mandy reached for the bay window platform. She came up a bit short and, instead, unknowingly depressed an extended piece of white trim, which opened an eighteen-inch concealed drawer. Having heard his girlfriend fall, Zak hustled to the living room and turned on a light, where he found Mandy staring at the $200,000 he had secretly stashed.

"Oh my God, Zak! How much money is in there?"

"It's from the pub," Zak explained. "I didn't have a chance to make it to the bank this week."

Mandy wasn't buying Zak's story. "You couldn't have made that much money in a year. What are you, Zak, a drug dealer?"

Zak feigned outrage. "I've never done or sold drugs in my entire life!" I'm telling you, there's not as much money there as you think. It's just proceeds from the pub."

"Don't lie to me, Zak! Business has been good, but not this good."

Zak knelt down, pushed the drawer closed, and wrapped his arm around Mandy. "Look, it's my money. I've earned it. It's not as much as you think, and a chunk of it I'm using to repay the loan to my uncle."

"Alright, Zak," Mandy relented. "I get it. It's your own damn business."

Zak took his girlfriend's hand and pulled her from the floor. "Come on. I'm still tired. Let's go back to bed."

—

Gavin Fitzgerald looked over his right shoulder, then drove a rundown Ford from the Eighth Street curb outside Milwaukee HIDTA. "Who are we on our way to speak with?" Garrett Marks asked.

"Two weeks ago, I had the IFC. (Intelligence Fusion Center) look up Mookie's cell phone number, and asked them to locate his phone. Unfortunately, he was smart enough to keep his location services off. Nonetheless, I subpoenaed his cell phone records. The bad news is Mookie dumped his phone. Still, I found a series of calls made to him from one particular number in the days leading up to the phone being dumped. The IFC identified the owner of that phone as Xavier Davis. I have a hunch Davis is aware of Mookie's whereabouts. If Mookie talks, we'll know who ripped off Trey's stash house on Lynx Road."

Fifteen minutes later, Fitzgerald depressed a white button inside the vestibule of a north side apartment building. "Who is it?" a voice over an intercom asked.

"Detective Fitzgerald from the Milwaukee Police Department." A second later, the occupant buzzed the door open, and the detectives made their way to a second-floor unit.

"Over here," the apartment's occupant shouted when he spotted the investigators. "Step on in. I've got some nosey neighbors always tryin' to get in my business."

"Are you Xavier Davis?" Fitzgerald asked.

"Yeah, that's me."

"Do you have any idea why we're here?"

"Well, yeah, probably about my cousin."

"And is your cousin Dinkins Danbury, also known as Mookie."

"Yeah, sure was."

"What do you mean, 'sure was'?" Fitzgerald asked.

A puzzled look appeared on Xavier's face. "You mean, y'all don't know?"

"Know what?" Fitzgerald asked.

"Mookie's dead. He got killed down in Atlanta. Man, I thought the cops there sent you over here to shout at me about it."

"When did you first hear about this?"

"About an hour ago," Xavier answered. "My Auntie Bell from Atlanta called me about it."

"Did she say what happened?"

"She said Mookie got killed by a car, and the police wasn't sayin' much more about it."

"Well, I'm kind of curious why Mookie was in Atlanta," said Fitzgerald. "Was he having problems here?"

"Mookie said a drug dealer's crew was out lookin' for him. He stopped over and wanted to borrow some money to leave town so he could stay at our auntie's house in Atlanta. So I gave him two hundred dollars, and then drove him to the train station. He asked me to check on his crib while he was gone, but, when I stopped over there, the place was turned inside-out."

"In regard to who was looking for him, did he mention any names?"

"Not that I remember. Mookie said something about some money. Look, detective, my cousin ran with a rough crowd, but he was tryin' to keep it straight. He's blood, so I did what I could to help him out. I don't know what happened down in Atlanta, but, if you want to find out, the police there know more than I do."

———

"Gavin," clerk Jennifer Flores shouted across the room, "you have a call on line one — Atlanta homicide."

"This is Detective Fitzgerald."

"Hello detective, this is Lieutenant Marcellus Weatherby, Atlanta PD homicide, returning your call. I understand you may have some information regarding the Danbury homicide."

"Homicide," Fitzgerald said, "that's news to me. I was told Mookie was killed in a motor vehicle accident."

"He was killed by a vehicle, after fleeing a building where he had apparently been tortured. He was tied onto a chair with large sheets of plastic wrap, managed to escape with the chair still on his back, and ran out into a busy street with one of those cheap football helmets on backwards. We're scratching our heads down here looking for answers. I was hoping you might be able to help us out.

"We suspect one of local narco gangs was looking for him," Fitzgerald explained. "The word is they suspected Mookie of giving another group the location of one of their stash houses that was robbed. The thing is, we're still uncertain who Mookie was working for."

"We've had some luck checking on the warehouse where he was tortured. It's owned by one of our problem landlords, who has rented it out in the past for raves and women's jello wrestling. He claims a black male sought to lease the warehouse for a month to store some items he planned to have shipped to Milwaukee. Unfortunately, when the building's owner took the rent money and turned over the keys, he didn't photo copy the Wisconsin ID. He believes the man's first name is Kevin, and described him as six-foot, thin, medium complexion, mid-to-upper- twenties. For all we know, the ID could have been purchased on the dark web. We're seeing more and more of them lately."

"If you would like," Fitzgerald offered, "I could overnight the booking photos of the crew that was looking for Mookie. They may come in handy for photo arrays."

"Thanks you. That would be helpful. Whoever was interested in Mr. Danbury was obviously trying to get something out of him. They tortured him by placing a lit cigarette on his genitals."

Fitzgerald cringed. "Ouch, that had to hurt. My guess is the perpetrators were looking for the names of those who did the rip. I'll get those photos together and get them in the mail before the day's end."

CHAPTER EIGHTEEN

Shaniqua Barkley sat patiently in a black Lexus inconspicuously parked in the rear of a restaurant located a half-block north of the Milwaukee Police Department's Wisconsin Avenue evidence retention center. A man in a tan jacket and blue jeans approached the Lexus, opened the door, and sat in the front passenger's seat. Barkley handed the man an envelope containing five thousand dollars. "Here's the phone," said Matt Wittig, a property control officer with a gambling problem.

In turn, Barkley gave Wittig the same make, model, and color cellular telephone. "Here's the replacement. You sure you can make the packaging look like it wasn't messed with?"

"I'll do my best," Wittig replied, as he placed the envelope and cellular telephone inside an interior coat pocket, left the car, and entered the restaurant for lunch.

The off-duty sergeant reached for a cell phone and called Trey Downing's sister. "I got the package in the mail. I'll be bringing it to the spot."

Unknown to Barkley and the property control officer, the cell phone — allegedly recovered from Maurice Bruce — doubled as a GPS tracking device. The meet had also been videotaped by an FBI agent in a nearly Dick's Plumbing truck.

Fifteen minutes later, when Barkley turned the cell phone over to Trey's enforcer, a high resolution camera, attached to the bottom of a small plane hovering above, captured the matter. The sergeant then drove to District Seven for the start of her shift. As she retrieved a duty bag from the trunk of her car, two FBI agents approached from the rear. "Sergeant Barkley, Geoff Fisher with the FBI. We need to talk."

Inside the Wisconsin Avenue warehouse, Officer Matt Wittig donned a pair of latex gloves, slipped the replacement cell phone inside a previously marked plastic bag, and carefully heat sealed the bottom opening. A small camera, surreptitiously placed in the ceiling during a fire drill, watched as Wittig replaced the inventoried evidence.

Whisked away by the two agents, Barkley was directed to call in sick. She was then driven to a hotel room in suburban Wauwatosa, where she was given an ultimatum: wear a wire to gather evidence against Trey and his crew or spend a half-decade in prison. The weeping sergeant agreed to the latter.

In the interim, the GPS tracker and the small airplane kept tabs on the cell phone as it was taken inside the Hopkins Street clubhouse. "Let me see that phone," said Downings, who reached for a hammer. "Time to bust this damn thing up."

———

After the dinner rush at The Fallen, Ethan set a plastic cup of diet soda and ice on the end of the bar. "Busy again tonight," the bartender told the head cook.

"Yeah, but we cranked it out," Raul replied, as beads of sweat rolled down his forehead.

Ethan surveyed the immediate area to ensure the pub's customers were out of ear shot. "Did Zak fill you in on Mandy?"

"No, what's up?"

"She literally stumbled upon his money," Ethan reported. "She thinks Zak's a drug dealer."

Raul shook his head in disbelief. "Oh, that's not good. She's just one argument away from snitching him out. What does Zak have to say about it?"

"He's attached to Mandy," Ethan explained, "and actually believes he's convinced her the two hundred large is proceeds from the business."

"Come on, Scrap. He can't be that stupid."

"We both know Zak's not stupid. The problem is he's thinking emotionally, and not with his head."

"So," Raul asked, "what are we going to do about it? Our asses are on the line here, too."

"The four of us need to meet," Ethan asserted. "We need to form a consensus. Can you make it to Matty's on Monday at 1700 hours?"

"Sure thing, Scrap. It's one of my days off, so it'll work."

"Okay, then. I'll let the others know."

———

Having awoken unusually early, Zak threw back a cup of joe at Mavis' coffee shop. Running a tad late, Xavier walked through the door at fifteen minutes after seven. "Sorry I'm late. I got stuck in traffic."

"No problem," Zak said. "So what's up with Mookie? When we first talked, you said he had been hit by a car. What's changed?"

"At first, the police wasn't saying much, just that Mookie was hit by a car. Then, my auntie called and said, whoever did it stuck a cigarette in Mookie's nuts; that Mookie ran out of a warehouse buck-ass naked with a chair tied to his back, bolted out into traffic tryin' to get away and got killed." Tears formed in Xavier's eyes. "Trey's boys got to him. It's all my fault."

"Whoa, whoa, whoa," said Zak, seeking to smooth over Xavier's guilty feelings, "let's slow things down for a minute. Why do you think Trey's boys were involved? Mookie was living on the edge, right? How do you know Mookie hadn't crossed some goons down there?"

"Well, even though the police aren't sayin' much, it sure sounds like something Trey's boys would do. I'm tellin' you Zak, we should kill those bastards."

"You want us to start a war with a homicidal street gang, even though we have no proof they're actually involved? That's crazy, Xavier. I know this is tough on you, but you need to calm down. The detectives that come into the pub talk about their cases. If Trey's people killed Mookie, they'll hear something. Until then, cool off a little."

"You know my auntie's got no money," Xavier explained, "so I'm gonna have Mookie's body brought up here and pay for the funeral."

Zak put his right hand on Xavier's shoulder. "That's a good thing you're doing, giving the man a decent send off. He did us right. I'll kick in a thousand to help pay for the wake."

Xavier wiped the tears from his eyes. "Thanks, man. That means a lot to me."

"I've also got some problems of my own," Zak said. "Mandy found my money — all two-hundred thousand."

"Damn, Zak, what you gonna do about it?"

"Nothing for now. I told her the money was from the business."

"What did she say? Did she believe you?"

Zak nodded affirmatively. "Yeah, I think so."

—

Garrett Marks read through a stack of transcribed conversations from the Stewart Street bar. "These goofs actually believe the dope was planted in Musty's truck."

"Either Musty has Nero's Ignitors totally buffaloed," ATF Agent Vance Rathman speculated, "or he's telling the truth, and the coke isn't his. That sticky note on the cellophane packaging seemed too good to be true. When I was a kid, my dad told me if something seems too good to be true, that's because it probably is too good to be true. And the anonymous caller, a Hispanic-sounding male who used a one-time, throw away phone, kind of makes me believe there's more here than meets the eye."

"Regardless, we've caught a few interesting tidbits on the wires," Marks added, "like the boat being used to run heroin to Michigan."

"True, and that'll help the DEA. Yet I'm kind of disappointed we've heard nothing about the Greendale bomb."

"The wires have been up for just a few days," said Marks. "Give it some time."

As the two investigators talked shop, Jennifer Flores handed a letter to Marks from the Wisconsin Regional Crime Lab. Marks opened the envelope and carefully read the contents. "Some good news, Vance. The crime lab found Musty's DNA on the outside of the coke's cellophane packaging."

"What kind of DNA?"

"Saliva," said Marks.

"Kind of unusual for a dope case," Rathman theorized. "Still, it's going to be tough for Musty to explain it away. Maybe I was wrong, and it was Musty's dope after all."

After the lunch hour rush, Raul flipped through the pages of a newspaper left at the bar by a customer. On page eight, he spotted a byline, El Nino's to Close One Location, in the business section. "The Milwaukee ethnic Mexican food chain El Nino's," the article noted, "is closing its underperforming South 27th Street location," said the company's managing director Hector Manuel Pina. "Management informed the store's ten full-time employees and thirty part-time employees of the closing Friday."

El Nino's must have some thin profit margins, Raul thought, as he waved The Fallen's owner over. "Hey, check this out."

Zak glanced through the article. "Wow, the entire operation is apparently being kept afloat with dope money."

"I feel bad for the workers, though," Raul sighed. "They didn't do anything wrong."

"This is precisely what happens when a business expands too quickly and overextends itself," Zak opined. "And, worse yet, uses dirty money to underwrite the expansion."

Had Raul or Zak watched the prior night's local evening news, they would have caught wind of the arrests of three men — Juan Rafael Matos, Miguel Domingo, and Ernesto Cuellar — for several counts of armed robbery. According the criminal complaint, Cuellar told investigators the three had been given two months to repay a Mexican drug cartel four hundred thousand dollars "or else." Although Cuellar, citing concerns for his safety, declined to provide specific details, News 50 reported the defendants had worked at El Nino's.

CHAPTER NINETEEN

Attired in a white dress shirt, a fashionable, black necktie, and black slacks, Ethan entered The Fallen's side door, hung a navy blue dress coat on a rack, and walked behind the bar. "Good crowd tonight, Zak, and it's still early."

"Business has picked up since the weather's turned cooler," Zak responded. "Hey, before you get started, I need to talk to you in the basement." Zak stuck his head through the service window in the kitchen. "Raul, can you watch the bar?"

"Sure thing, man."

Ethan followed Zak down a flight of steps. "Not sure if you've heard or not," Zak explained, "but our plan worked. Mookie is no longer with us."

"Do you know the details?"

"Based on what Xavier has told me, it sounds as if the 4-5's attorney passed along our info. They went down there, abducted Mookie, and took him to some type of warehouse. He got away, ran out in traffic, and was hit by a car. Xavier suspects Trey's crew. The police haven't arrested anyone."

"So far, so good," said Ethan. "So how's Mandy holding up? Has she said anything else about the money?"

"Nothing, nothing at all. She's going to stop in anytime now."

After returning to the main floor of the pub, Zak replenished the shelves with bottles of high-end liquor, while Ethan, who had just finished mixing a slew of drinks, caught a glimpse of Mandy as she entered the side door. Ethan reached for a coaster and went to the far end of the bar. "Good evening, Mandy. You're looking good tonight. What can I get you?"

"Thank you, Ethan. How about a cosmopolitan?"

"One cosmo it is."

In short order, Ethan mixed the drink in a shaker and set the glass in front of Mandy. "You're in early tonight. Do you have any plans?"

"I just thought it might be a good idea to get a better look at this operation," Mandy said sarcastically. "Apparently, this place is a license to print money."

Yeah, right, Zak, Ethan thought, Mandy has said nothing about the money.

When Zak finished stocking the shelves, he glanced to his right and spotted Mandy at the end of the bar. As Zak chatted with his girlfriend, three women in their mid-twenties entered the front door, placed coats over their seats, and bellied up to the bar. Ethan retrieved three coasters and greeted the customers. "Good evening, and welcome to The Fallen. Would anyone like something to drink?"

"How about three vodka presses," an attractive brunette, wearing a low cut, strapless, blue blouse replied.

"Good deal. I'll be right back with the drinks."

As he rang up a tab, Zak looked to his left and caught a glimpse of the woman in blue seated at the bar with her friends. Hailey Chevallier flashed a smile, and Zak went to greet her. "Hailey, you're back in town."

"I came home for the weekend for my nephew's birthday. Zak, these are my friends, Emma and Rachel."

"Nice to meet you."

"This summer, when my car wouldn't start, Zak helped me out," Hailey told her friends. "The place looks great."

"Thanks. My dad is a finish carpenter. He put in a ton of work."

Ethan tapped Zak on the shoulder. "When you get time, could you grab a couple of bottles of Prangle's from the basement?"

"Sure thing, Scrap." Zak then turned to the three women. "I've gotta get to work. Stick around and we can talk later."

On his way to the basement, Mandy grabbed Zak's right arm. "Who is that?"

"Who's what?" Zak asked.

"The woman you were talking to over there," Mandy sneered. "That floozy wearing that flimsy, blue blouse when it's freezing outside."

"Her car broke down outside last summer. I helped her out and had it towed to the shop. It's the first time that I've seen her since."

Zak retrieved the two bottles of vodka from the basement. When he returned, Mandy had just finished her second drink and had ordered a third. "Slow down," Zak whispered to his girlfriend. "Pace yourself."

"Don't tell me to slow down," Mandy snapped. "You're the one that should slow down and spend more time with me." With the Saturday crowd packing the pub, Zak didn't have time to argue. He went to the center of the bar and began filling drink orders.

Thirty minutes later, Garrett Marks and Alex Reyes walked through the side door, and put their coats over the two remaining seats at the bar, which happened to be adjacent to Mandy's. "Oh, shit," Zak mumbled, as he spotted the two off-duty detectives seated to the left of his slightly, inebriated girlfriend. With two coasters in his right hand, he went to the end of bar and greeted the new arrivals. "Alex, Garrett, what brings you in on a Saturday?"

"We went to the basketball game," Reyes replied, "and thought we'd stop for one on the way home. Busy night, huh?"

"Busier than a one-legged man in an ass kicking contest," Zak joked.

"Is this lovely lady your significant other?" Marks asked.

"She sure is. Mandy, this is Garrett and Alex. They're with the Milwaukee Police Department."

"The police department," Mandy mused, "how interesting. What do you do there?"

"We're detectives," answered Marks. "I investigate the bikers and white supremacist groups. Alex is guy who investigates money laundering."

"Like drug money?" Mandy asked, as she glanced toward Zak.

"Drug money, gambling proceeds," Reyes explained. "Any illicit funds that are run through a business to cover up illegally obtained income."

Not missing a beat, Garrett Marks removed an item from his wallet. "Here's my card. If you ever see or hear something, give me a call."

"Ohhhh, I'll do that," Mandy replied, as her speech began to slur.

Out of the corner of his eye, Ethan spotted Mandy chatting it up with the two off-duty investigators. Holy shit, Zak. Get her away from them, he thought.

Fortunately for Zak, the detectives were more interested in socializing with his tipsy girlfriend than talking shop. "Besides hanging out with Zak, what do you like to do for fun?" Marks asked.

"Zak," Mandy shouted, as she pushed her empty glass forward, "can you get another drink for me?"

Zak handed the empty glass to Ethan. "What the hell are we going to do?" Ethan asked.

"Mandy can't handle her liquor. She's already slammed three cosmos and is slurring her speech. Make this a strong one."

Ethan mixed the drink in a shaker, then walked to the glass to the end of the bar. "Thank you, Ethan," Mandy shouted. "At least you've got some class." Mandy took two large gulps, then placed the glass on the bar. Zak watched as the color faded from her face.

"So," Reyes asked, "how did you and Zak meet?"

"I, I, I," the inebriated woman hesitated, "I'll be right back." Mandy made a beeline for the women's restroom, dropped to her knees, and vomited in the toilet. When she emerged from the restroom, beads of perspiration, which had fouled her makeup, slithered down her face.

Zak stepped around the bar, put his arm around Mandy, and turned towards Reyes and Marks. "I think she's had enough for tonight. This is what happens when you drink on an empty stomach."

"Fuck you, Zak," Mandy mumbled.

"Come on, Mandy. Don't embarrass yourself," Zak whispered. "I'll take you upstairs so you can sleep it off." With his girlfriend in tow, the couple disappeared through the pub's rear door.

A short while later, Zak returned to the bar. "Is she alright?" Marks asked.

"She's fine. I don't know what got into her tonight," Zak reasoned.

"Been there, done that," Reyes chuckled.

At the other end of the bar, Ethan talked things up with the three attractive women. "Was that Zak's girlfriend at the other end of the bar?" Hailey asked.

"It is," Ethan replied, "but they're kind of on the outs. Everyone knows it, except Zak."

"We have to run to meet some people downtown," Hailey explained. "Would it be okay if I left my new number for Zak?"

"Sure, I'll pass it along to him," Ethan said.

Hailey removed a pen from her purse and scratched down her number on the back of a drink receipt. "Now, let him know, if he doesn't call, I'll understand."

"There's a lot of unhappy people at El Nino's," said Javier Marquez, as he sipped from a bottle of beer in Raul's living room. "They can't believe their spot got hit."

"Who do they think did it?" a curious Raul asked.

"At first, they thought it was a crew hooked up with the dude who owns the building, but, that didn't checkout. All they got is two guys dressed like Jewish ministers and a black dude, who pretended to be an electrician."

"Could be people from out of town," Raul theorized.

"Who knows, but it's kind of strange. El Nino's crew is real tight, but none of the dudes who did it were Latino. Now they're thinkin' the cops."

"That's crazy," Raul replied. "Why would they think it was the police?"

"Because one of the Jewish dudes was talking to a cop in a police car right in front of the building before they left in a van."

"How do they know that?" Raul asked.

"One the crew from El Nino's was bringin' back some food and saw it. But you know how it is: it's not like they can call the cops and ask."

Raul shook his head in disgust. "So, they got away, clean, huh?"

"The moving truck they boosted was found parked over at Jones Island," said Marquez. "So they're checking around the south side. If they find out who did it, man, they're in for a world of hurt."

Inside Matty's bar, Dwyer fetched a pitcher of beer as Raul, Ethan, and Xavier gathered around a small table. "Man," Xavier nervously muttered, "I'm not getting a good feeling going behind Zak's back."

Having heard the remark, Dwyer sought to tap down any talk of going soft. "If Mandy talks, the cops will take a long look at Zak's books and realize the numbers don't add up. At a bare minimum, the feds could prove money laundering, which means they'd seize his money, his business, and maybe even his car. Unless, of course, he has something to offer."

"And that something is us," Ethan interjected.

"If something happens to Mandy," said Raul, "Zak's going to know one, or all of us, is behind it. How do you think he's going to deal with it?"

"Look," Ethan said sternly, "based on what I know about Zak, if he wasn't emotionally attached here, he'd come to the same conclusion: the problem needs to be dealt with. Before we go any further, let's take a vote: all in favor of dealing with Mandy, make your intentions known."

"I'm in," said Dwyer.

"Damn, this is a tough call," Xavier remarked, "but put me down as a yes."

"Raul?" Ethan asked.

"I'm definitely a no," Raul replied, as he looked his three colleagues straight in the eyes. "I signed up to fuck over the dope man, not this bullshit."

"If we move ahead," Ethan asked, "will you at least help us get the ball rolling? I promise that all you'll need to do is attend group tomorrow night and stop here with the rest of the group afterwards."

"I can do that," Raul responded. "And, although I don't agree with what's going on here, I understand that we all will sink or swim together. So you can count on me to keep my mouth shut."

"Look, man. I've lost a lot," Xavier added. "My cousin's dead, and the dudes who did him, well, they're still out there. We all have to make sacrifices. It's not pleasant, but, the way I see it, now its Zak's turn."

"Okay, so we're all good here," Dwyer remarked. "Scrap and I have talked this over, so listen up."

"Mandy's been trying to get Zak to attend one of your vets' group meetings for over a month," Ethan explained, "but Zak purposely stays a little late before taking off on Tuesdays to ensure he can't make it. I'll put a bug in his ear that he may want to smooth things over with Mandy by attending tomorrow night's meeting. Raul and Xavier, all you have to do is attend like you normally do. But afterwards, you gotta get Mandy and Zak to have beers with you here."

"What good is that going to do us," Xavier asked. "Are you going to off her here, right in front of Zak?"

"Let the man finish," said a grimacing Dwyer.

"The key is, that once all of you are here, to get Mandy to leave by herself."

"But she'll want to leave with Zak," Raul noted.

"If things go as planned," Ethan insisted, "and I think they will, she'll leave in a huff. Look at the three cameras inside this place. If you stay here with Zak, the cameras will show you couldn't have been someplace else. Meanwhile, I'll be working the bar, which means all of us affiliated with the vet's group, and yours truly, have alibis."

Dwyer leaned forward and placed his elbows on the table.

"That leaves me — the only person unaccounted for on a Tuesday night — to resolve the problem."

"That also means Zak's going to know who did it," Raul reasoned.

"I know everyone here thinks the world of Zak," Dwyer said, in a cold, cunning voice, "but I think the man's a pussy. Just follow the plan and do your part. I'll deal with Zak."

———

Seated on a comfortable, black leather sofa, Trey Downings handed a glass of Champagne to Shaniqua Barkley. "You did good, girl. Whatever pictures of me that Mo Mo had on that phone, they're gone now. Did your cop friend appreciate the donation?"

"Donation?" asked the wired Barkley, in an effort to decipher the code for potential jurors. "Oh, you mean the five thousand dollars?"

"Yeah," Trey clarified, "the fuckin' money."

Barkley laughed. "He probably already blew through that shit at the casino."

"What a stupid fuck. I should have just gave it to the Indians myself."

After a knock, a man standing guard opened the rear clubhouse door, and two tall men dressed in all black entered. Trey stood up and slapped one of the man's hands. "Gino, what you got for me, brother?"

"Just twenty-five big ones," Gino answered. "It's the end of month, so it's been kind of slow."

Trey smiled. "That's alright. In two more days, it'll be the first of the month when Uncle Sam shits. Then, those fiend motherfuckers will be lined up outside ATM's at one minute after midnight to get their money. Alright, it's cool for now. I'm chillin' with Shaniqua, so I'll see y'all tomorrow."

Gino motioned to his silent sidekick, and the man standing guard opened the rear door that led out to 37th Street. As Gino crossed the threshold, a loud blast shattered the otherwise quiet night. Gino collapsed to the ground. As he gasped, in pain, for air, the hole in his chest made a noticeable wheezing sound. Armed with an SKS rifle, the guard went outside, checked the area for intruders, and provided cover as Shaniqua Barkley ran to her car before the police could arrive.

———

LeRon Meeks donned a pair of purple latex gloves. He lifted a yellow tarp just enough to get a look at the dead body resting on the cold sidewalk in the rear of the Hopkins Street clubhouse. "More gang shit. Why do we have to catch so many of these damn gang cases?"

"Just when we're making progress on the Ivey homicide," said Nick Cortes, "one of Trey's boys gets sniped. Name's Gino Pendergrass, a twenty-eight-year-old felony offender. Mostly dope stuff."

Meeks cracked open a steno pad. "Have the coppers come up with anything?"

"We've got a thirty-two-year-old female witness with twenty-twenty vision," said Cortes, looking down at his notes, "who said she saw a red Dodge Durango pull away from the curb in front of her second-floor apartment a hundred feet to the north. It was dark, but she believes the sole occupant was a well-built, black male."

"How sure is she on the vehicle's make and model?" Meeks asked.

"She said one of her 'babies' daddies has a black one just like it."

"Well, it's something," said Meeks. "How many red Dodge Durangos do you think are in Milwaukee?"

Cortes' eyes looked upward. "Hell if I know. I'm guessing a few hundred."

Meeks smiled. "That's not too bad. I've got court in the morning. After I punch in, I'll get on the horn and order a list of red Dodge Durangos registered to addresses in Milwaukee County from the D.O.T. (Wisconsin Department of Transportation).

CHAPTER TWENTY

As he surveyed the street from his living room window, Ethan glanced at a piece of paper, and then made a telephone call. Two rings later, a female answered. "Hello."

"Hello, is this Hailey?"

"Yes, it is."

"This is Ethan. I'm the bartender at The Fallen. The other night you asked me to pass your number to Zak."

"Okay," Hailey responded cautiously.

"The reason I'm calling is I want to surprise Zak. He's part of a vets' group that meets on Tuesdays. Afterwards, they go out for a few drinks. After you left, Zak said he really liked you a lot, but didn't have the nerve to call — something about being snake bit."

"Oh," said Hailey, "I think I know what that's about."

"So, I thought, why not ask you to stop by the bar where they meet." Ethan suggested. "You know, like you simply went to the place and Zak just happened to be there. I'm sure he'd like to see you. He said a lot of nice things about you."

"He did?" Hailey asked. "Hmm, well, I guess there'd be nothing wrong with just popping in. What's the name of the place?"

"Matty's, it's on fifty-eight and Vliet. It's a typical corner bar. Nothing special, but the beer's cheap."

"About what time?"

"The meeting is usually over by eight," Ethan explained. "Maybe eight-thirty."

"Alright, I'll ask a friend to tag along."

"Hailey, just one thing. Please don't tell Zak I called. If he found out I got involved and set this up, even though I know he really likes you, I think he'd really be pissed off. Since he's my boss, that wouldn't be a good thing."

"Okay, I won't mention it."

"Thanks, I appreciate it. And, afterwards, if you and your friend are interested, stop by The Fallen. I'm bartending until close and will buy each of you a drink."

————

Summoned to a meeting at Milwaukee HIDTA, Lieutenant Maureen Donnell and two of her detectives, LeRon Meeks and Nick Cortes, took seats on the same side of a conference room table. Gavin Fitzgerald, and FBI Agents Geoff Fisher and Monica Wright, sat on the opposite side, along with Captain Steve Jordahl.

"The reason we asked the three of you here," Jordahl explained, "is to discuss the ongoing investigations of Trey Downing's crew. Maureen, from reading the reports, I see LeRon and Nick have made significant progress on the Ivey homicide. Gavin has debriefed Bruce, but, since his credibility as a testifier will be challenged, the FBI has found an avenue to gather additional evidence. Even though you may be able to implicate some of Trey's crew in the Ivey homicide, we're asking that you two keep doing what you're doing, but hold off on taking the case to the DA's office."

"While LeRon and Nick have done a great job," Donnell replied, "holding off won't be a problem. The case still has some holes, primarily who the actual trigger man is."

"When our investigation wraps up," Fisher explained, "we should be able to fill in those gaps."

"What has complicated matters," said Jordahl, "is Pendergrass getting killed by the sniper. The FBI's work will take more time. I believe the extra wait will prove worthwhile. The question is how long can we hold off if the tit-for-tat retaliation spills out into the streets? These things have a way of taking on a life of their own. If the media begins hyping a gang war, the chief and the mayor will want arrests made to show something is being done."

"Look," Fitzgerald added, "I was in the middle of the 4-5 Mob investigation when I got sucked into the vortex created by Trey's crew. I only have a few more months left on this project, and would like nothing better than to indict Trey's crew and tie it all in with the 4-5's. Still, what kind of window are we looking at here?"

"Our best guess is three months," said Wright, as she reviewed a series of spreadsheets. "We have a lot of phone records and other documents to look through. Then, if things work out, the grand jury process will create additional follow up."

"I know homicide is busy," said Fitzgerald. "So I'll make time to search through records and locate witnesses."

———

Doc Moreau looked around the room. "I thought we had a very productive meeting again tonight. Zak, it was nice to see you again. It sounds like your business is keeping you focused."

"Thanks, Doc," Zak replied, as Mandy smiled and reached for her boyfriend's hand.

"Then," said Moreau, as he stood from his chair, "I'll see you here in a couple of weeks."

"Zak," Raul shouted, "are you two stopping at Matty's?"

"I don't know," Zak said. "I'm kind of beat."

"Come on, Zak," said Mandy, in a demanding tone of voice. "We never socialize together. And some people who come to the meetings, like Xavier, haven't seen you in a while."

"Okay, okay," Zak relented, "we'll stop at Matty's."

After leaving the church, Zak accompanied Mandy to her car for the short, two-block ride. When the couple arrived at the bar, they pushed two small tables together. A short time later, Raul retrieved two pitchers of beer and poured the contents into eight plastic cups.

"So, Zak, how's the business been going? Xavier asked.

"Super good. You should stop in sometime."

Fifteen minutes later, as the conversation at the table turned to events in the news, Zak left for the restroom. Hailey and her friend, Rachel, entered Matty's and took seats at the bar. When Zak returned, Hailey immediately spotted him. "Zak, how are you?" Hailey moved closer and gave Zak a hug. "What a surprise seeing you here!"

Seated with her back to the bar, Mandy turned just in time to witness the embrace. She walked towards her boyfriend and tapped him on the back. "So you haven't seen her since summer, huh? Fuck you, Zak, find your own way home. I'm leaving."

"Wait a minute, Mandy. There's no need to leave…"

"Forget it, Zak. Don't touch me. I'm leaving!" Mandy grabbed her jacket and stormed out the front door.

"Ah, well, ah, I'm sorry if I…," an embarrassed Hailey stammered.

"Forget about it, Hailey. It's no big deal. I don't know what her problem's been lately. Since you're here, you might was well join us."

Having witnessed the brouhaha, Xavier turned to his left and whispered into Raul's ear. "Think that was Scrap's doing?"

"No doubt," Raul confirmed. "The man's is a conniving genius."

Instead of driving straight home, a highly-agitated Mandy stopped at Mudslinger's, a corner bar on South 60th Street in nearby West Allis. She removed her jacket, placed it over a bar stool, and took notice of the tavern's other patrons — two intoxicated middle-age men at the far end of the bar. A bartender with a two-day-old beard, dressed in a tattered, black t-shirt, and ratty blue jeans, approached the most attractive customer the bar had seen in sometime. "Hello, young lady. What can I get you?"

"A Jagger bomb, please."

The bartender walked to the far end of the bar to retrieve the ingredients. "What's her deal?" one of the drunken men asked.

"If I were to guess," the bartender deduced, "I'd say a man problem."

"Never know these days," said the second drunk. "Could be a woman problem. Two-to-one says she's a lesbian."

In short order, the bartender brought Mandy the drink, which she consumed in three large gulps. She then placed a twenty dollar bill on the bar and shouted, "I'll need another."

Twenty minutes later, as Mandy sipped from her third drink,

she reached into her purse and removed the card given to her by Detective Garrett Marks. I know how to get back at that creep, she thought. After taking a gulp from her drink, Mandy entered the first three digits of Marks' number, thought better, and deleted the call. She then slammed the remainder of the drink. "You can keep it," she shouted to the bartender, in reference to the change. The buzzed woman then made her way out the door and to her car for the three-quarter-mile drive home.

Less than five minutes later, Mandy pulled into an alley just north of 63rd and Mitchell Streets, drove fifty feet east, and pulled her car into a parking stall in the rear of a two-story bungalow. She stepped from the car and, back lit by an alley light, made her way to the building's rear door. In the quiet of the night, she heard a noticeable creak-like sound coming from a dark nearby gangway, and stopped in her tracks. Frightened by the noise, Mandy stared into the blackness for a full five seconds. After starting for the door, she heard a thump, collapsed to the ground in excruciating pain, reached for her stomach, and felt an arrow.

Under the cloak of the gangway's darkness, Dwyer folded a light, fifty pound, pistol-grip cross bow, placed the object in the front waistband of his pants and zipped his jacket. As his body raced with adrenaline, the masked man moved passed the moaning victim to the alley. Before emerging from the alley onto 63rd Street, Dwyer removed the ski mask, placed it inside a jacket pocket, and donned a black ball cap.

In a panic, Mandy did the worst thing possible: she wrapped her hands around the shaft of the arrow and attempted to remove the projectile from her abdomen. A horrifying scream awoke neighbor Dave Paskiewicz, who went to the rear door of his home, stepped onto the porch, and heard a woman in the yard to the west groaning. "Oh God, someone please help me!" Paskiewicz went to his kitchen and retrieved a flashlight. After returning to the porch, he was shocked to see the young neighbor he barely knew, lying on her back in a jacket soaked in bright red blood, with an arrow buried in her belly.

Paskiewicz ran back into his kitchen and called 9-1-1. "Can you grab towels, anything you can find, and apply direct pressure to the wound?" the operator asked. He pulled open a kitchen drawer, grabbed two dish towels, and ran out the door. "Oh shit, this really hurts," Mandy moaned. Paskiewicz placed the towels around the wound. Within a matter of minutes, a fire truck and a squad car arrived. All Paskiewicz could do was watch as firefighters tried to save the woman's life.

Soon, a slew of red and blue lights penetrated the night. Four EMT's quickly placed Mandy on a gurney and whisked her to the rear of a med unit. Having been told the injured party had lost a lot of blood, a young West Allis police officer climbed inside the rig to speak with the victim. "Who did this to you?" the officer shouted. "Tell me, who did this to you?" Mandy struggled mightily to form some a single word. "Ah, ah, ah, ah," was the only declaration the officer was able to document before she slipped into shock and lost consciousness.

———

Garrett Marks turned off the small light on his office desk, reached for a jacket, and was set to leave for home when his cell phone rang. "This is Detective Marks."

"Hello, detective. This is Lieutenant Scott Kapanski, with the West Allis PD. We're over at Froedtert Hospital investigating a homicide. Do you, by any chance, know a white female named Amanda Wede?"

"Hmm," Marks thought for a few seconds, "I can't say I do. Why do you ask?"

"Ms. Wede was found with an arrow in her stomach in a backyard near 63rd and Mitchell. She has since expired. One of my officers searched her purse and found your business card."

"Is she affiliated with the bikers?" Marks asked.

"We're still in the process of doing a work up on her, so I can't say one way or the other. Any chance you could meet me at Froedtert?"

"I'm on my way. I was about to head out for the night. The hospital is on my way home."

Marks left the office, climbed inside his personal car, and drove west on I-94. He arrived at Froedtert Hospital twenty minutes later, entered through the emergency entrance, and went directly to the trauma center, where he spotted a group of West Allis police officers congregating in the corner. "I'm Detective Marks, from Milwaukee. One of your lieutenants asked me to meet him here."

"Lieut," one of the officers shouted, "the guy from Milwaukee is here."

Kapanski waved Marks over. "Though you indicated the victim's name didn't ring a bell, would you be willing to take a look at the body?"

Marks shrugged his shoulders. "Sure."

The lieutenant pushed a large, silver button, which caused two heavy doors to swing open. The investigators entered the trauma room and walked to a corner. Kapanski pulled open a sky-blue ceiling curtain. Several tubes remained in the dead woman's arms and mouth, and the arrow was still embedded in her belly. "Yeah, I know her," Marks remarked, "but I know her as Mandy. She's the girlfriend of the owner of a bar called The Fallen. The last time I was there, she was in some sort of tiff with him, got drunk, and had to leave."

"And what is the boyfriend's name?" the lieutenant asked.

"Zak," Marks answered. "Zak Klatter."

Coming soon: the second of Mitchell Nevin's *Nico's Warrior's* trilogy. To check for updates or to comment on the book, visit @ nicoswarriors at Twitter for updates.